DARK CONFLICT

Simon Merrivale owns a mask and headdress, and the legend is that whoever comes into contact with them will find their body taken over by the long-dead Shaman at full moon. Merrivale is dragged from his home, and he and the relics are taken to an isolated mansion. There, Ernest Caltro and his followers prepare to conduct a Black Mass with Merrivale as its human sacrifice. Can Simon's friends Richard Blake and Stephen Nayland mount a rescue mission?

JOHN GLASBY

DARK
CONFLICT

Complete and Unabridged

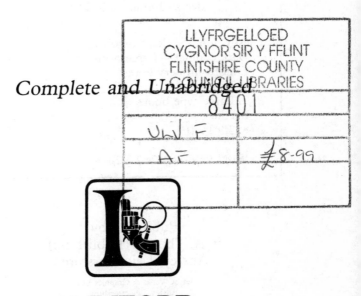

LINFORD
Leicester

First published in Great Britain

First Linford Edition
published 2008

British Library CIP Data

Glasby, John S. (John Stephen)
    Dark conflict.—Large print ed.—
Linford mystery library
    1. Horror tales
    2. Large type books
    I. Title
    823.9′14 [F]

ISBN 978–1–84782–220–8

Published by
F. A. Thorpe (Publishing)
Anstey, Leicestershire

Set by Words & Graphics Ltd.
Anstey, Leicestershire
Printed and bound in Great Britain by
T. J. International Ltd., Padstow, Cornwall

This book is printed on acid-free paper

1

Journey into Evil

The plane banked steeply, came down over the London airport through swarming clouds which seemed to press in on all sides, cloaking the ground below until it was only dimly seen. From the air, whenever it was possible to see through the storm, London looked like a toy city sprawling out over the landscape, then it began to expand rapidly as the plane went down.

Stephen Nayland sat at ease in his seat, feeling the seat belt tighten momentarily around him as the note of the straining engines altered subtly. Beside him, the tall figure of Richard Blake, legs thrust out straight in front of him, stirred slightly.

'What does it look like out there?' he asked

Nayland shrugged. 'Pretty thick,' he said. 'We may have some difficulty getting into the city unless the fog lifts a little.'

'I've arranged for a hire car at the airport, but if the fog thickens we may not be able to use it.'

'Maybe you'd better put me into the picture fully,' Nayland said. 'There may not be another chance before we reach Merrivale's place and I don't want you to have to do any explaining to me in front of him.' There was a slight silence as the other peered out of the window of the plane at the yellow fog that seemed to hold them in a never-ending cloud of pale yellow light.

Then Blake said briefly: 'I know you've spent almost a couple of years on that remote Scottish island in the Hebrides and you may be wondering why it was so urgent I should go up there to see you myself. The point is that I needed to see you to get your opinion first without having to drag you all the way to London if my fears are completely unfounded.'

'Go on.'

'There isn't much more to tell. Most of it I've simply pieced together from the few facts I've been able to learn. If I'm right there may not be much time as far as Merrivale's concerned.'

Nayland sat tautly upright in his seat, feeling the odd little vibrations of the plane running through his body, reaching up into his brain, scratching oddly at his nerves. 'Go on,' he said thinly.

'I had a letter from him a couple of weeks ago. It's been quite a while since he last wrote which, in itself, is unusual for him. Usually, he lets me know how things are going on every week or so.'

'And what he mentioned in his letter made you think that there's something fishy going on at his place?'

Blake shook his head. 'It was what he didn't say in his letter that worried me. I got in touch with you as soon as possible. You've had more experience with this kind of thing, since that strange happening in Egypt a year ago.'

'You think it's as bad as that?'

'Maybe. It seems he's been taking up these evil rites with some — dangerous — people. He tried to pass it off as a joke in his letter, but I pride myself on being able to read between the lines and I'm

3

afraid it's something more than just a joke. He's in it right up to the neck. He's also aquired an acient African mask and headdress. He says he bouhjt it in some old curio shop in London, some place tucked away in one of the backstreets.'

'So?'

'I haven't seen it myself but I've heard of the shop where he got it and my guess is that it's the real thing — one of those the Shamans used during their horrific rites.'

'Have you any idea why he might have done such a foolish thing and put himself into the hands of these people?'

'He's a strange man at times,' Blake said. 'I've been watching him closely during the past couple of years. I think he fell in with them because he felt that he was empty inside, that there was very little purpose to his life. Since that accident eighteen months ago he hasn't been able to get around very much as you know. He misses all of the old excitement.

'I used to see quite a lot of him whenever I was in London. I suppose you did yourself. But he abruptly terminated

4

his visits to me, and any invitations for me to visit him, a little over four months ago.

'He believed that he had some other goal in life, something extremely important. He didn't tell me what this goal was, but at the time I suspected it was just another fantasy. From what I've been able to piece together, I gather that he's finally moved completely into this evil world.'

'If he has, we may find it difficult to bring him back. Black Magic is all right if you treat it lightly and know when to get out, but if you take it at all seriously and get into it too deeply, they'll never let you go without a fight.'

'Then you believe with me that he's in danger?' Blake looked at Nayland sharply.

'It's possible. I'll know better once I've met him and had a talk with him.'

'Maybe he won't want to see us.'

'Then we'll have to force our way into him.'

Outside, the ground came up suddenly, flashing past the plane with an incredible swiftness as the wheels touched the ground.

As the plane stopped, Nayland unfastened his seat belt quickly and stood up. There was a tense feeling of alarm growing in the pit of his stomach, but he kept his face expressionless as he turned to face the other. 'Let's get to that car you've got waiting. I've got a feeling in my bones that things won't wait for long before something breaks.'

★　★　★

The winter evening was dark and still and filled with a faint washing of rain that came drizzling down through the fog. But apart from the rain beating like tiny fists on the glass, streaking the windows, and the purring of the engine, there seemed to be an absolute silence that wrapped itself around them, eating into Nayland's body.

He tried vainly to concentrate on what Blake had told him on the plane. If what the other had said was anywhere near the truth, there might be little they could do for Merrivale. Why the devil had the other been so foolish? Surely he could have seen where all this was bound to lead. It wasn't as if he was a child who didn't understand these dark things.

He peered out of the car window. It was difficult to see the wet surface of the road and yet his companion at the wheel seemed to have no difficulty in finding his way through the maze of streets which passed them on either side, half seen in the swirling mist.

Nayland shuddered inwardly although he didn't quite know why. There was something awful about to happen. He had no idea what it would be, but he knew with a strange sort of inner conviction that it would happen in spite of everything he could do.

He had the strangely persistent idea that there was something dark and horrible waiting somewhere for him in the very near future, just out of sight at the moment, but lurking there with a patient stillness, ready to leap forward and overwhelm him at the first opportunity.

He sensed that Blake was thinking and feeling the same, despite the unerring way he was guiding the car through the darkness and the swirling mist.

The utter quiet and stillness around them seemed to be peopled with soundless, half-noticed things that flitted on the very edge of his vision, moving swiftly and noiselessly in the silence. He found himself sweating a little in spite of the chilliness of the night air.

Fiercely he controlled his mind. Perhaps once they reached Merrivale's place in the city and had a straight talk with him, these ghosts that peopled his imagination would fall into their proper perspective and he would find himself laughing at them.

But maybe, his mind persisted, something really was wrong and there was something waiting for them that was not of this world, lurking in their path, knowing by some strange sense that they were coming.

'Well,' said Blake suddenly, 'we're nearly there.' He spoke with a forced cheerfulness. 'Now we'll soon get to the bottom of this mystery.'

The car moved over to the side of the road and the tall buildings became more distinct. The fog seemed to have thinned a little during their journey, or perhaps it was because they were a little nearer to the river and there was a slight breeze blowing off the water.

Blake's features were pale as the car stopped outside one of the houses. Switching off the engine, he fumbled a little nervously with the door of the car as he got out and stood waiting for Nayland.

Nayland looked towards the windows where a square of yellow light showed through the fog.

'I never mentioned to him that we were coming,' Blake said. 'I thought it might be best if we dropped in on him unexpectedly. If he knew we were coming he'd see to it that we discovered nothing.'

'Best way,' agreed Nayland, 'but it looks as though he's got company.'

'That's a pity,' Blake said. 'He won't thank us for breaking in on him at a time like this if he has guests. But I'm ready to gatecrash his party if you are. I dare say the worst he can do is to have us thrown out.'

Blake stood for a long moment, staring up at the gaunt shape of the building. The single light in the window seemed to stare down at them through the swirling fog like an evil, unblinking eye, watching their every move.

'I've tried to put myself in Merrivale's place,' he said finally, 'but I still can't figure out why he did such a stupid thing as this.' He stared up at the tall building, as though trying to see through the walls into what lay beyond.

'Simon Merrivale isn't a fool,' Nayland said. 'He hasn't gone into this thing with his eyes shut, but that isn't the same thing. These people are far more danger-ous than we give them credit for. They make things seem so easy and innocent at first. If God won't give you the things you want, and the things that you think you ought to have, then why not ask the Devil for them? At first, it's all so tremendously exciting.

'It gives you a sense of power and there are few men in Merrivale's position who can resist that. It isn't until later that you realize just what kind of a black web of evil you've woven around yourself.

'By that time, you're in it so deep that you can't get out. Besides, you've already seen something of their power and it isn't long before you realize that their weird mumbo-jumbo really works. They can do these things they've boasted about. In fact, they can kill you quite easily if you refuse to carry out their orders.'

In front of the house that was set back from the road by a short gravel drive, were big hedges and trees of evergreen that had been carefully clipped into the shapes of animals after the Italian style. Beyond them, at the end of the drive, three stone steps led up to the front door.

The windows that looked out on to the street had a sense of aloofness about them that gave an added touch of dismal grandeur to the place and the immense front door, beneath the rounded stone arch, was of oak banded with iron.

They crossed the narrow terrace without speaking and stood in front of the tall door. There was a grotesque metal knocker that Nayland raised and then allowed to fall so that the echoes chased themselves through the corridor beyond before losing themselves in the distance.

'God, what a place,' said Blake hoarsely. 'I always get the creeps whenever I come here. Why Merrivale keeps it on beats me.'

Nayland nodded. The heavy knocker, a hideous bronze head, a Gorgon's face, distorted and ugly in its reality, with widely staring metal eyes, stared at him with a terror that was somehow beyond life.

There was a long silence. All around them the stunted bushes and dryly whispering leaves seemed to mutter warningly.

Nayland's head jerked abruptly. The sound of heavy footsteps shuffling along an echo-ringing passage, reached their ears. A wooden board creaked behind the door.

Then a lock rattled and there was the sound of a heavy chain being drawn back. Nayland glanced at Blake out of the corner of his eye. Something was wrong when their friend, Merrivale, had to lock his door like this at such an early hour.

The door swung open on protesting hinges and Nayland saw a tall, bulky figure outlined against the flood of yellow light. It was impossible to see the details of the man's face in the shadow, but he had the unmistakable impression of eyes boring into his own with a penetrating stare.

'Yes?' There was a question in the other's voice.

'We'd like to see Mr. Merrivale,' said Nayland harshly.

'I'm afraid that won't be possible, sir. Mr. Merrivale has very important guests this evening. He left word that he wasn't to be disturbed on any account.'

'Then I'm afraid that we must insist.' Nayland spoke sharply. 'However important his guests are, it is more important that we speak with him now.'

'Tomorrow, perhaps,' said the man-servant.

'Tonight,' said Nayland tensely. The feeling that something was terribly wrong suddenly crystallized in his mind. He propelled himself forward, jamming his foot inside the door as the other attempted to close it in their faces.

'Now take us to Mr. Merrivale right away, otherwise I won't answer for the consequences.'

'This is highly irregular.' The man-servant's voice was a sibilant whisper, 'but I'll find out whether Mr. Merrivale can see you. If you'll just wait here for a moment.'

He led them into the long, thickly-carpeted hallway. Hanging along its walls were trophies of past safaris in African jungles and the plains of India. Nayland stood perfectly still, looking about him.

Everything seemed normal. As far as his memory served him, nothing had been altered since he had last visited this place almost a year earlier.

But in spite of the unchanged appearance of his surroundings, there was an undercurrent of insidious warning that he noticed immediately, something which sent little thrills of ice spilling up and down the muscles of his back. The difference in this place was subtle, but horrible.

He turned to Blake. 'Don't you feel

something odd about this place?' he asked suddenly.

'Odd?' The other looked puzzled.

'It's just a feeling I've got. Strange I've never noticed it whenever I came here earlier.'

'I don't sense anything different. It's just the same old place as far as I can see.'

Nayland ran a finger along his cheek. The little germ of suspicion in his mind began to grow, tightening into a tiny knot of apprehensive fear in his chest.

Everything about him was suddenly ominous. This long hallway with its heavy curtains over the windows, drawn so tightly together so as to deny them even the slightest glimpse of outside — that manservant, obviously a foreigner of some kind, whom he had never seen before — the way the man had tried so deliberately to get rid of them as if there was something taking place here about which they ought to know nothing.

A door creaked noisily somewhere in the dark distance and a faint mutter of conversation reached his ears. A moment later there was the sound of slow, hesitant footsteps approaching the door at the end of the hallway. It opened suddenly and there, looking out at them with an expression of surprise on his heavy, fleshy features, stood Merrivale.

He came forward slowly and extended his hand.

'Why, Nayland — and you too, Blake. This is a surprise, but it's good to see you after all this time.' There was a strained tone of forced geniality in his voice. His lips twitched into a thin smile, but it never reached his eyes.

'Sorry we burst in on you like this, but we didn't realize that you had important guests,' Blake said.

'Oh that's all right.' The expression on his face showed both embarrassment and fear, thought Nayland.

'I was told that you wanted to see me about something of the greatest importance,' Merrivale went on, his eyes averted. 'Are you sure that it won't wait until tomorrow? I'm afraid I can't leave my guests for long.'

Nayland looked at him directly. 'This isn't like you,' he said quietly. 'We've never kept any secrets from each other in the past.'

Merrivale stared back at him, his face suddenly expressionless. 'Secrets?' he repeated. 'But there's nothing like that. It's simply that I've arranged a very special party for my guests and they'll be — annoyed — if I don't go in to them.'

'I'll bet they will.' Nayland took a step forward towards the partly opened door 'Just what's happening through there, Merrivale?'

The other stepped back swiftly and placed himself squarely in front of the door. He gave a nervous smile.

'There's nothing happening, Nayland. Now be a good fellow and call back again tomorrow. If I'd received any warning of your coming, I might have been able to invite both of you. After all, you are my closest friends, but as it is I'm afraid that it's impossible now.'

'I think I'm beginning to understand,' muttered Nayland, jerking his head towards the door. 'It would be fatal to invite us now because then you'd have more than the required number. Is that it?'

'I'm afraid I don't know what you mean,' said Merrivale thickly. There was a tenseness about his stance which Nayland noticed instantly. It had been a shot in the dark as far as he was concerned, but it had struck home. *So he hadn't been wrong!*

'Then let me see what's going on in that room.'

Merrivale hesitated, then allowed his arms to fall limply to his sides and stood away from the door. All resistance seemed to have been drained out of him.

Quickly, Nayland pushed open the door and stepped through. The fear began to come back with a rush. He turned savagely on Merrivale. 'You fool! You utter, goddamned fool. Getting yourself mixed up in something like this. How deeply are you involved in it?'

He felt suddenly sick in his stomach. There was a clock chiming eerily somewhere in the far distance, the strokes standing out as individual sounds in the weird stillness. But it was the interior of the room that held his attention. At first, he could scarcely believe what he saw.

The entire floor of the room had been taken up and then replaced by small marble slabs of different colours laid in a queer, cabalistic design that was terrifyingly familiar, set in the middle of the floor. He felt his nostrils begin to close at the pungent smell that pervaded the entire room. It was an odour he couldn't quite place although he had the idea that it was vitally important for him to recognize.

In the very center of the marble floor, set in blue and red slabs, was a vast, many-sided figure with a weird tracery of signs around it. Tiny crystal cups glittered at the corners of a five-pointed star and these, he noticed, were filled with a clear, colourless liquid.

With an effort, he thrust down the rising tide of revulsion in his brain. The impulse to turn, to grab Merrivale by force, and hustle him out of this accursed place into the car outside, was almost more than he could control.

But that wouldn't solve the long-term trouble, he reflected soberly. If anything, it would have the opposite effect, that of pushing Merrivale further into this unholy mess. The other could be both obstinate and pig-headed whenever he felt like it.

He turned slowly to say something to the other but at that precise moment, a thick oily voice said softly: 'More guests of yours, Mr. Merrivale? Why don't you invite them in to join the party? I'm sure they'll both find it extremely interesting.'

Nayland whirled. Someone stepped out of the shadows directly into the light of the hallway. The man was short in stature, but the way he held himself and the broadness of his body made him appear taller than he actually was. He was wearing a dark blue robe that reached almost to the floor, covering a tailored dress suit.

But it was his face that held Nayland's attention. Broad and fleshy, stamped with a faintly cruel expression, with deep blue eyes that dominated his features. Nayland could feel that gaze boring into him uncomfortably.

With an effort, he forced himself to meet it. Here, he thought, was the danger — for there was death and evil in this man's eyes.

2

The Mask of Darkness

Merrivale stood in the background looking acutely uncomfortable. Nayland watched him out of the corner of his eye. The other seemed ill at ease, his face twisted into an expression of indecision.

'We're all ready to begin,' said the dark man, turning to speak to Merrivale. He seemed to have forgotten the others' existence completely. 'But before we do so, don't you think you ought to introduce us?'

Merrivale looked up quickly. 'Why — yes, of course. This is Stephen Nayland and Richard Blake — Ernest Caltro.'

'I must confess that I overheard a little of what you were saying a few moments ago, Mr. Nayland,' said Caltro smoothly. 'I see that you understand a little of what we are trying to do, but that you don't agree with our work.'

'I only know that what you're about to do is unutterably evil,' said Nayland carefully. At the moment, there was no reason to antagonize the other. But if it ever came to a showdown —

Caltro smiled blandly. 'I'm sorry you have such a bad opinion of us, we don't deserve it really, you know. All we are seeking is knowledge. But as your friend has already told you, we are about to begin our meeting and,' — he glanced down swiftly at the watch on his wrist — 'it is important that we begin right on time. If you'll forgive us.'

It was more of a statement than a question and Nayland realized that somehow the other was beginning to gain control of the situation, to turn things to his own ends.

But that was something that must not be allowed to happen. He racked his brain to think why tonight, of all nights, should be so important to these people. Clearly they were preparing for something big. This was going to be something more than the usual meetings they carried out.

Then it came to him. November the seventeenth! Merrivale's birthday. The most potent day for anything of this kind. Other little things began to slip into place, all adding up inside his mind. It was also the night of the full moon, although he had forgotten this completely since there had been no moon that evening because of the fog that shrouded the entire city.

He spun on his heel and faced Merrivale. Perhaps there was still time to talk the other out of his intentions.

'Listen, Merrivale,' he said harshly. 'I beg of you not to go through with this tonight. If you have to fall in with their plans, at least put it off until tomorrow so that we can have a good long talk beforehand. I'm only telling you this for your own good, believe me.'

'But I don't see that I can. I mean — ' Merrivale paused helplessly.

'What my friend is trying to say is that everything has been most carefully prepared,' said Caltro silkily. 'It will be impossible to postpone it, I'm afraid. Completely out of the question. I'm quite sure that Mr. Merrivale appreciates the consequences if he fails to go through with this.'

There was an undertone of menace to the other's flat voice and his face seemed to have hardened momentarily.

'Damn you, Caltro,' snapped Nayland sharply. 'Do you think that I can't see through your little scheme? I've met your kind before, not only here but all over the world. I know you for what you are.'

Caltro smiled. There was a curious look in his deep-set eyes as though some hidden demon had leapt up at the back of them and stared out into the world, naked and terrible. Then the expression was gone.

'I'm afraid that you must know very little about me, Mr Nayland,' Caltro continued smoothly. 'Otherwise you would know that I am a man who goes through with a thing once he has started it.' His features hardened. 'But enough of this talk, we have work to do and time is getting short.'

He glanced across at Merrivale and almost immediately the other said apologetically: 'I'm afraid I must ask both you and Blake to leave right away, Nayland. I'll see you tomorrow around nine o'clock if that'll suit both of you.'

There was an expression of pleading in his grey eyes that was not lost on Nayland.

'Very well. If that's the way you want it,' Nayland shrugged. 'It's your house and your party but I beg of you to reconsider what you're about to do. It may seem exciting on the face of things, but underneath it's both rotten and highly dangerous. These are evil people. They won't stop until they've made you one of them and by that time it will be too late for anyone to help you.'

'I know what I'm doing, Stephen,' muttered the other stiffly. He moved towards the outer door, waiting for them.

Nayland looked across at Blake. 'Let's go,' he said curtly. 'There's nothing more we can do here.'

'I'm glad you realize that, Mr. Nayland,' said Caltro in his thick oily voice. There was a look of malignant triumph on his broad features.

Blake hesitated, his right hand clenched

into a tight fist, then he stepped forward quickly. 'By God,' he hissed savagely, 'if you're trying to get Simon into your clutches. I'll kill you myself.'

'Careful, Richard, careful,' warned Nayland hoarsely.

Merrivale closed the door behind them as they stepped out into the drizzling rain. The mist seemed to have thinned appreciably and there were only a few swirling streamers still clinging to the houses and around the lights

'Are you going to leave Merrivale back there with those fiends after all?' asked Blake sharply as they got into the car and pulled away from the pavement into the middle of the road.

Nayland shook his head. 'Not if I can help it,' he muttered grimly.

'Then what do you intend to do?'

'I'm not quite sure at the moment. There was no sense in creating a scene back there with that creature looking on. He was enjoying every minute of it.'

'But you still think that Simon's in danger?'

Nayland pursed his lips. 'He's in

terrible danger,' he said hoarsely. 'By that, I don't mean that they'll injure him physically, but they'll take over his mind, utterly and completely.

'By the time they've finished with him, he'll be totally under their domination. Nothing that we or any of the psychiatrists can do will be able to alter that.'

'But damn it all, Stephen. This is modern-day London. We aren't living in the Dark Ages now. Then, I can quite see the superstitious people believing in such things as Black Magic and vampirism and all the rest of the mumbo-jumbo. But not now, surely.'

'What difference do you think the century makes?' said Nayland with a sharpness beyond his intention. He felt suddenly more on edge than ever before. 'The worship of the Devil is as old as Christianity at least. Probably far older. And you wouldn't say that that had died out, would you?'

'No. I suppose not, but — '

'Try to remember this, Richard. There are always two sides to every road, just as there are two sides to life itself. There's the black and the white — the good and the evil. Both of them are always with us, no matter how hard we try to escape them and both are dangerous forces to be reckoned with.

'Believe me, I'm not speaking without some experience of these things. If you'd seen as much horror and terror as I've witnessed during the past fifteen years or so, you'd realize why it's so important to get Simon away from those fiends tonight.'

Blake rumbled out a low laugh. He seemed tensed, but tried to look at ease as he leaned back in his seat. The sound of the tires on the wet surface of the road hummed in their ears.

'I thought when I wrote you that letter that there was something going on at Merrivale's. Maybe there is, and I'm prepared to admit that this fellow Caltro is a pretty good actor when it comes to scenes like that we had tonight, but the idea that he can really take away a man's soul is ludicrous.'

'Never underestimate these people, Richard,' Nayland said quietly. 'That could quite easily be fatal. I've seen what they can do to a man and believe me, it isn't nice.'

'Then what do you think we should do? We can't come here and take him away by force. That manservant looked a damned tough customer and no doubt there are more of them ready to pitch into us if we start any trouble. And we can't very well go to the police and say: Look, there are some Black Magicians trying to steal the soul of one of our friends. They'd lock us up before we knew where we were.'

'That's true, of course,' Nayland nodded. 'That's one of the reasons I decided to leave when I did. They were on their guard then, ready for any move we might make. But somehow, I don't think there's much danger to Simon until midnight. That's when they'll reach the culmination of their ceremony. It's up to us to break into his place without being seen and try to take them by surprise. We'll both go armed, of course just in case, although it's possible that guns won't be of any use against what we might run up against in there.'

'I'm with you. When do we leave?'

Nayland checked his watch. 'There's plenty of time,' he said flatly. 'We don't want to rush into anything with our eyes shut. Besides, did you notice anything strange in the hallway tonight?'

'No — It looked exactly the same as it always did.'

'That's what I thought at first. It wasn't until we were leaving that I noticed the object hanging above the door of the far room in which they were holding their fiendish ceremony.'

Blake looked puzzled. 'I don't remember seeing anything unusual,' he said. 'That is, apart from the usual trophies Merrivale's been collecting for as long as I can remember, but that was all.'

'Not quite. There was one trophy there that I don't recall ever having seen before. It took my attention immediately I noticed it. The Shaman's headdress and mask. Lord knows where he got it from, but unless I miss my guess, it must have been stolen from some tribe and brought back here to London.'

31

'Oh — that.'

'You've seen it before?' Nayland asked, genuine surprise in his voice.

'He showed me it the last time I visited him. That must be almost eight months ago. He said he'd picked it up in some odd curio shop he stumbled across somewhere in the back streets of London. But what's so important about that?'

'Perhaps nothing. Perhaps everything. But I've no doubts whatever that it's the genuine article he has. I'd say that thing contains more evil than all of Merrivale's other trophies put together. I only hope that Caltro hasn't recognized its importance.' The car reached one of the main streets and pulled into the main stream of traffic. The two men sat silent; Blake because he could think of nothing more to say, and had to concentrate on driving, and Nayland because he was, once more, absorbed with his own thoughts and fears. He felt a trifle uncertain, not sure whether he was doing the right thing or not in proposing to go back and try to take these people by surprise.

'You know, we could be letting ourselves in for a lot of trouble if you're wrong, Stephen,' said Blake suddenly. 'Simon made it perfectly clear to us that he didn't want to see us again tonight and, after all, he is thirty-eight, when he ought to know his own mind and make his own decisions.'

'I always seem to do foolish things on the spur of the moment. Maybe that's why I'm still alive and sane. And we've got to make our move tonight: do you realize what day it is today, as far as Simon's concerned?'

'Today?' There was a question in Blake's eyes, then he gave a little start. 'Why yes, it's his birthday. I'd forgotten all about it. And you think this has some bearing on what is happening tonight?'

'I'm sure of it. If they intend to make him one of them, to get him to cross the Abyss, then today is the most potent day of the year for that purpose. Everything is right for it. The stars have returned to the positions they had on the day he was born. The signs are extremely favourable.'

He checked his watch again. It was a little after eleven o'clock.

'We'll go along to my flat and pick up a couple of revolvers,' he said tensely. 'By that time, we'll be ready to go back.'

3

Something Evil

The house, resting in darkness behind drawn curtains, seemed deserted and sound asleep. Nayland moved forward slowly, watchful and alert, aware of Blake beside him.

The storm that had been hanging over the city for almost three hours had moved away into the distance and although lightning still flashed along the northern horizon, the sky overhead was almost clear of clouds and moonlight splashed a brilliant patch of spreading light across the moist earth that lay between them and the nearest window — making things doubly difficult in case they did have someone watching for them to return.

It was impossible to tell whether they had fooled Caltro or not. Nayland had the impression that nobody could read what went on behind those impassive features.

He stood silent for a long moment. An owl hooted, somewhere close at hand, muttering a throaty warning among the trees. Somewhere in the distance a church bell chimed the quarter hour, the echoes faint and far away.

Nayland found himself shivering slightly, uncontrollably.

'Not a sign that there's anyone there,' whispered Blake softly. 'No lights in any of the rooms.'

'Maybe they've drawn the curtains over them so that nothing shows.' Nayland shrugged his shoulders noncommittally. 'Either that, or they're no longer here, but somehow I don't think so.'

Carefully, they made their way round to the rear of the house, retreating into the shadows, moving through the thorn bushes that edged the lawn. Something slid away through the undergrowth, shrieking a thin wail of fear as it scurried across a patch of moonlit grass.

Nayland's pounding heart stopped beating for a moment. But it was only a cat. A half-starved, mangy creature that fled for the darkness as though all the devils in hell were on its heels. With an effort, he steadied himself and forced his heart into a slower, more normal pace.

Little thoughts were buzzing around in his head like flies. It was extremely likely that they were fools coming out here at this time without making any real preparations. They weren't up against ordinary people now, he reflected. These people possessed terrible powers of darkness that he had witnessed not once, but many times in the past. If anything went wrong . . .

A few moments later, they reached the rear of the house and paused in the shadow of the trees before going forward again. On the face of it, the place seemed deserted. No lights. Not a single sound. But it had that odd waiting quality hanging over it and he had the feeling that eyes were watching them out of the darkness, following their every move.

He had the chill sensation that they were walking directly into a nightmare; that the high walls in front of them and the tall trees all around them on either side, formed a clinging shell and there was nothing on the other side of it all but death and fear and utter horror.

'Can't see a damned thing out there.' Blake's words reached him eerily from the moon-thrown shadows.

'We'd better break in through one of the windows,' whispered Nayland. He paused and looked carefully about him, hugging the shadows of the trees. 'And we'll have to be careful. There's no telling what fiendish things we may find in there. Keep close behind me and do whatever I tell you without asking any questions.'

'I understand,' Blake said thinly.

'Good. Then come on. But no noise! If that man Caltro should once suspect that we're here — '

They reached the back of the house, pressing themselves tightly against the cold stone of the wall. All of the windows had heavy curtains drawn across them and several were crisscrossed with strong steel bars.

Death and evil are out here, Nayland reflected suddenly, and all of the things usually associated with, and part of, the night.

A chill came over him as he stood there; a chill not so much from the cold night air, as from a subtle something that tore at his nerves. His body felt taut and his nerves were stretched to breaking point.

He turned his head a little and tried to shut out the low, moaning murmur of the wind as it rustled through the branches of the trees. Somehow, there seemed to be a voice in it that gave him a sick, empty feeling in the pit of his stomach. It was a terrible, dismal voice, lonely and vast and far away. A voice which spoke to him of Death, a last gasping breath, a screaming of torture, of Hell itself.

'There's nothing here,' said Blake quietly, after a brief pause. 'If there was we ought to have — '

'Quiet!' hissed Nayland sharply, clutching at his companion's arm. 'I thought I heard something. There!'

'I don't hear anything.'

'Listen.'

For a long moment, there was complete silence; an eerie stillness that dragged on and on until Nayland began to think he had been mistaken. There was the thin, white mist still hanging around the house and in the darkness he couldn't see anything plainly, but the blackness seemed to do something to the smallest noise, magnifying it, distorting it a little until it was scarcely recognizable for what it really was.

And then, from somewhere inside the silent house, there came the insistent throbbing that he had heard a few moments earlier. It seemed to be coming from a long way away, a monotonous thudding like a drum being beaten in a hollow, echoing room.

'Hellfire,' Blake muttered, starting forward, 'what the devil is it?'

'I don't know. But whatever it is, I think we have to find out.'

Nayland worked his way slowly along the wall until he reached one of the windows without the steel bars across it. He gave the catch a cursory glance and then took a long, slender-bladed knife from his pocket.

The window creaked in protest as he inserted the steel blade beneath the framework, prizing it gently upwards with slow, steady movements of his fingers. His grim features were tight with concentration.

A moment later, the blade snapped upward, breaking the lock. Nayland slipped the knife into his pocket, then eased the window silently upwards, revealing a square of darkness within which nothing moved.

'This is it,' Nayland said quietly. 'Keep close to me and don't make any noise.'

Gingerly, he pulled himself up by his arms and eased his body through the window. Touching the floor with his feet he pulled himself upright and moved back a couple of paces, feeling behind him with his hands like a blind man. In his mind's eye, he could see Caltro and the rest of these fiends, sitting somewhere in the darkness, possibly within a few feet of where he was standing at that moment, watching him.

Blake's dark shadow appeared in the opening, outlined against the night. A moment later, he dropped gently down beside him and stood breathing heavily in the dimness.

Carefully, Nayland stepped forward into the darkness. The silence was broken only by the continuous dripping of a leaking tap somewhere close at hand and he figured that this must be the kitchen. In the darkness, it was almost impossible to see anything and until he was sure of his bearings, he didn't want to use the torch in his pocket.

On the other side of the kitchen, furthest from the window, he found the door. It opened quietly as he twisted the handle, but the darkness beyond it was blacker still. He stopped for a moment and held his breath, motioning Blake to remain quiet. Still nothing moved.

He was just beginning to think that the house really was deserted and those people had decided to take Simon Merrivale away to perform the ceremony elsewhere; a place where they wouldn't be interrupted, when he heard the noise again. It was appreciably louder now.

A monotonous thudding that appeared to come from somewhere near the top of the house; sharp, drumming echoes that chased themselves through the stillness.

Carefully, Nayland took the pencil torch from his pocket and snapped it on. Midnight shadows twisted and scurried away from the light as he played it around the walls of the narrow passage in which they found themselves. He stood quite still for a full minute, thinking back, recalling the general layout of the house. At the moment, they were at the rear of the place.

Finally, he was satisfied. At the end of the narrow hallway, he found a half-open door and opened it slowly. Beyond it lay the large room in which they had earlier seen the intricate marble design with the huge altar against one wall, ready for some hideous ceremony to take place.

The room was empty. Huge grotesque shadows moved around the massive shape of the altar as he played the beam of the torch over it. The long black candles in their silver sticks stood out in startling detail.

But where were Caltro and Merrivale and the other participants they had not yet met?

The luminous hands on Nayland's

watch showed that it wanted only another six minutes to midnight. Little bits of half-forgotten knowledge were filtering into his mind, forcing their way into his consciousness.

Whenever people became involved too deeply with Black Magic in its most terrible and potent form, almost invariably their minds were manipulated by people like Caltro. He did not doubt that this man was an Ipsissimus of the Order of the Left Hand Path and extremely dangerous. He had seen for himself the powers such people possessed, how they would promise anything, until susceptible men like Merrivale would fall entirely beneath their spell, heeding nothing but what was told them.

His fingers were beginning to tremble slightly as he walked cautiously forward into the vast room. The faint drumming sound continued to hammer away into his brain, but he could not locate where it was coming from.

At the far end of the room a stairway spiraled up to the rooms on the first floor. In the light from the torch, the stairs stood out in black and white, leading upwards until they vanished out of sight.

'Empty?' said Blake in a hushed whisper. It was more of a question than a statement.

Nayland felt his scalp tighten. 'I don't think so. I wish to God I knew where that drumming sound was coming from, and what it is.'

He led the way across the room and threw open a door set in the far wall at the side of the stairs. Blake heard his sudden sharp intake of breath a moment later and came hurrying forward.

'What is it?' he asked sharply.

'There — see.' Nayland swung the beam along the wall, until it rested just above the door through which they had just entered.

'I don't see anything.'

'Exactly. That mask and headdress were there when we came earlier. They've gone.'

'But what's the significance of that?'

'I only wish to God I knew. I've a feeling they've taken them away for some purpose. But where are they? Apart from

45

that goddamned noise, I'd say the place was completely deserted. But it isn't like them to have left in the middle of their ceremonies.

'Merrivale said himself that everything had been prepared and that they couldn't postpone it. Caltro would never agree to either stopping or postponing the ceremony just because we showed up and there was the possibility that we might return. Instead, I would have thought they'd have posted someone to watch for us in the event that we did come back.'

'Maybe we'd better see if there's anyone upstairs. That's the only place they could be. We've seen nothing down here.'

They went back into the huge room, their feet making no sound on the thick carpet that surrounded the marbled floor.

Boom — boom — boom! The sound continued to throb in their ears, unceasing, and it had a spine-chilling quality about it that set Nayland's teeth on edge.

Halfway up the stairs, he paused and slipped the heavy revolver out of his pocket, hefting it into the palm of his right hand. He could now sense danger all around them.

Boom — boom — boom — boom!

They reached the top of the stairs and stood quite still for a moment, looking about them, getting their bearings.

The drumming seemed to be all around them now, beating at them from all sides, great swelling waves of noise that thundered down at them as the weird echoes ran along the intersecting corridors.

Throwing all caution to the wind, Nayland suddenly cupped his lips and shouted at the top of his voice:

'Simon!'

There was no answer. Only the drumming seemed to increase still further in volume as though mocking him, scorning him for trying to pit his feeble strength against something far greater and stronger than he.

'Simon. Are you there?' Blake yelled the words at the top of his voice.

'Those fiends must have taken him with them when they left,' muttered Nayland harshly.

There was no need now for secrecy. If anyone were lurking in the house, they would know by now where they were. He had half-expected the drumming to stop once they had shouted and announced their presence in this way, but it still continued to beat and throb in huge murmurs of sound, rising to a mighty crescendo that filled the whole house.

'There's something wrong here.' Nayland led the way along the corridor, throwing open the first door he came to and snapping on the light. The room lay empty. The bed near the wall had not been slept in.

The second bedroom was almost exactly the same as the first; nothing had been moved, nothing seemed out of place. The room was sparsely furnished but everything was of the highest quality. Luxury seemed to abound in this place of mystery, he thought.

'Nobody there,' he said, glancing round to where Blake stood in the doorway. 'It looks as though the birds have flown and taken Simon with them.'

'But where could they have gone?'

Blake looked bewildered.

Nayland shrugged resignedly. 'One thing's certain. We'll never find them tonight.' He checked his watch. It was almost midnight.

A few moments later, the church bell in the distance chimed the hour, the long, drawn-out strokes sounding faintly through the moonlight. He shivered inwardly and began to count subconsciously. Many times in the past he had heard the Voodoo drums beating and booming endlessly in the tangled swamps of Africa and the West Indies.

He had watched the Leopard Men at their secret rites in the jungle, seen them on the prowl, seeking their victims, ripping and clawing at squirming, shrieking bodies, leaving them mutilated beyond human description.

But there had been times in the beginning when he had never believed. He had laughed with scorn at the curses thrown at him by the witchdoctors of the dark jungles of the African interior.

There had been other times when he had been forced to believe. When he had seen the walking dead as they had been summoned in a hideous trance that was neither life nor death but something unutterably horrible.

But here, somewhere in the heart of London, where everything should have been sane and normal, feeling the presence of unknown horrors ringing him around, all of the other terrors he had known in different lands among the more superstitious people of the world began to fade into insignificance.

Here, he felt, there was real evil. It wasn't the black horror of the voodoo or the chanted witchcraft of the jungles, the things he had been able to laugh at. Here, it was something different and far more horrible.

Some part of his mind, detached but alert, continued to count the slow beat of the distant chimes.

Five, six, seven . . .

He was suddenly aware that the insistent beating that had been with them ever since they had entered the house had suddenly stopped. When it had actually ceased its monotonous thudding, he wasn't quite sure. He stood there in the narrow corridor with the silent rooms on either side, sweating, feeling his heart thudding like a drum itself inside his chest.

He pulled himself together with a conscious mental effort. From the very edge of his vision, he felt sure he could see something moving at the far end of the passage, slipping in and out of the shadows, coming forward with a peculiar gliding motion.

Nine, ten . . .

He was suddenly aware that he was holding his breath and his knuckles whitened with nervous tension as he gripped the gun in his right hand.

For a second, nightmare was strong within him, pulling on the muscles of his throat so that he found it difficult to breathe properly.

Eleven, twelve . . .

Midnight! The sound of the distant chimes died away in tiny, shivering echoes in the moonlight. For a long moment there was complete silence, broken only by the gale of their breathing. Nothing seemed to move in the deep shadow pools of dark ebony.

And then, from somewhere close at hand, the air was split by the most horrible, piercing scream Nayland had ever heard. All of the fear and agony in the world seemed to be embodied in it.

A second later it ended in a long, drawn-out gurgle that was terrible to hear.

A moment passed. There was a queer look on Blake's face as he started forward along the corridor. A few yards ahead of Nayland, he paused. In front of them, a door clicked its lock and creaked open ominously.

Nayland turned quickly, the beam of the torch flashing along the walls. At the end of the corridor, he saw the door to one of the rooms beginning to swing slowly back.

There was a dim figure standing in the open doorway. A darker shape against the dim background. Nayland caught a brief glimpse of glittering eyes staring at him with a strangely hellish fury, and a leering grin that seemed to have all of the evil of hell locked in the curve of those lips.

'My God!' The words burst from Blake's shaking lips.

Nayland brought up the gun. The creature's outlines seemed crazily indistinct. At first, he could scarcely believe that it was a man. Then the other came closer and he saw the feathered headdress and the hideous mask.

At first, he could scarcely believe his eyes. The man was some kind of native, there was no doubt about that. But where had he come from and what was he doing here, alone in this house at this time of night? His first impression was that it was the manservant they had met earlier, but a second glance soon convinced him that this was not the case.

Breathlessly, he watched what happened next, scarcely conscious of the fact that Blake was standing less than five feet away. His mind was suddenly a screaming turmoil as the figure came closer, moving with stiff and inflexible steps as though in a trance. There was something madly familiar too.

What he was seeing was, of course,

impossible. Simon Merrivale? Now why should that thought rush through his head? He blinked his eyes several times. For an instant, he had the vague impression that the other turned and stared directly at him, watching with a look of grim, sardonic amusement behind the mask.

Nayland's body felt suddenly cold. Quite suddenly, he knew the gun in his hand would be futile and useless against this thing.

His hand was so limp that he could not raise it to aim and squeeze the trigger. Utter nightmare tore at his mind, trying to rip his brain to shreds. The creature moved closer, paused for a moment as it drew level with him and then moved on, down the stairs and across the room at the bottom.

It took all his failing will to keep from turning and running, screaming, down into the house, through the front door and out into the open, far away from this place. There seemed to be a thin, eerie laugh, high in the air, that trembled along his nerves.

4

Against the Darkness

'Merciful God,' muttered Blake, moving forward a little on shuffling feet. 'What the devil was that?'

'Steady,' Nayland said. 'We have to think and act calmly. Unless we do, we're both in terrible danger. This is something I never expected. I think we ought to go down there and see what's happening — if you're game to come with me.'

Struggling to control his nerves, Blake nodded silently and followed him down the stairs, occasionally mumbling words to himself that the other couldn't quite make out. They reached the bottom of the stairs and glanced about them. There was no sign of the thing which had passed them in the corridor at the head of the stairs, but it had to be somewhere in the house. Once they found that creature, he thought fiercely, they would get to the bottom of this mystery. He didn't know why he was so sure about that, but he felt certain that it would turn out that way.

As he walked forward, feeling the metal of the gun cold against the palm of his hand, he discovered that he was more afraid than ever before. It was a rising terror that seemed to fill the entire house and press down upon him as if the very air were solidifying.

There came a low, bubbling moan from just beyond the half-open door that led out of the room and Nayland, his left hand amazingly steady in spite of the fear that coursed through him, walked towards it and pushed it open with his palm.

Blake followed close on his heels as he shone the torch into the hallway. Shadows fled before the light and the mute heads of the animal trophies stared down at him out of temporarily glittering eyes as the light flashed over them.

'My God,' Blake pointed. Nayland steadied the beam and stared down at the still figure lying on the red carpet arms outstretched, legs doubled up beneath him.

'It's Simon.' Nayland threw a swift glance along the hallway before going down on one knee beside the inert body of Simon Merrivale, handing the torch to Blake.

'Here, hold this steady while I take a look at him,' muttered Nayland harshly.

'Is he — dead?'

'No. I don't think so. But he's in a pretty bad way. The sooner we get him away from here, the better.' He straightened his back and threw a swift glance around him Less than two feet from the unconscious man's outstretched fingers lay the feathered headdress and mask which had earlier been worn by that creature on the stairs.

'Do you believe in Black Magic now, Richard?' he asked grimly.

'I believe in what I see,' said the other tonelessly, 'and what I hear and what I can touch.'

'Still a materialist,' said Stephen. 'Then how do you explain what we saw back there?'

'I can't. But there has to be some rational explanation for it. There's no sign here of that creature we saw. Only Simon and it couldn't have been him.'

'No, it couldn't have been Simon. He's dressed in his usual manner. There would have been no time for him to have changed. There's no telling how long he's been unconscious. But why go to the trouble of leaving that headdress here?'

'Maybe it's Caltro's way of trying to scare us off,' suggested the other.

'I doubt it.' Nayland shook his head. 'There are plenty of other, more potent methods he could have used to do that. He wouldn't have to resort to trickery. No, there's something more to this than meets the eye.'

As he looked down at the feathered headdress and mask, Nayland began to feel uneasy. For one thing, a kind of cloudlike darkness seemed to hover around it; for another, there had been a similar cloud of darkness around that creature which had passed them at the top of the stairs.

At the same time, he was aware of an aura of evil that seemed to emanate from the mask. It was uncanny and profoundly disturbing. He was as conscious of it as he was of the fact that Blake was standing over him, looking down over his shoulder.

'Let's get him out of here,' said Nayland harshly. The mad panic was leaving him, but his heart was still hammering away madly inside his chest. 'If I hadn't seen it with my own eyes I'd never have believed it.'

Together, they lifted the unconscious man and carried him to the outer door.

Carefully, they carried Simon Merrivale to the car at the end of the short street and placed him in the back.

'You'd better ride with him just in case he comes round on the way,' said Nayland thickly. 'We'll take him to my place. He'll be safer there than anywhere else in London. Just in case Caltro finds that we've taken him and decides to come after him.'

'But what do you think is wrong with him?'

Nayland turned the key in the ignition and the engine started immediately. 'That's hard to tell at the moment,' he said wearily. 'They may have given him some kind of drug, that's their usual way of dealing with people if they give any trouble. On the other hand, it may be some kind of trance, it's difficult to say without having a good look at him.'

'Do you think you can help him?'

'I can have a damned good try,' Nayland said. 'If it's a drug he may need hospital treatment. If it's a trance, then we may be able to shock him out of it, but that will depend on how deep a trance it is.'

'What do you think happened to him?' Blake sounded puzzled.

'That's not easy to say. We can only make a guess at what occurred there after we left. For some reason they can't have carried out their ritual completely, otherwise they would have waited until midnight. Something must have happened to stop their plans. If only we knew what it was.'

'Maybe you were wrong about them from the very beginning. It could be that you were mistaken. I didn't see anything really evil about that man, Caltro.'

'Don't let his appearance or his

mannerisms fool you, Richard. That man is a devil in human shape. In true Black Magic there are a number of levels that can be attained by those who participate in it, rather like those in the Catholic Church. Once a member crosses the Abyss — as it's called — he becomes an Ipsissimus and take my word for it, such people wield powers you would never believe. I've met these people before and I know just what they can do.'

'So all right,' said Blake, watching Simon's unconscious body closely as though expecting to find the answer there, 'it's a case of Caltro either drugging Simon or hypnotizing him. What I want to know is, how long is he likely to be under their power, even assuming that we manage to keep him locked away from them at your place?'

'These things are not very easy to explain,' Nayland said. 'There's an old occult theory now generally being reaccepted by some, that thoughts themselves are as tangible as physical forces, that a thought of evil and hate can be a powerful enough force to act over a distance and affect anyone sensitive enough to receive it.'

'So that's all there is to it. All of the mumbo-jumbo which these people use, it's got nothing to do with devil-worship at all.'

'By no means. I said a thought of evil, remember? This is only one side to it all. There's the other, more deadly side to this horror. Devils, or demons, or whatever you like to call them are real entities that can be conjured up by people possessing the right knowledge. It isn't an easy thing to do, but it's as well to remember that people like Caltro control forces which are almost unknown to us.'

He concentrated on driving for several minutes before speaking again. 'That headdress and mask. It intrigues me. You say he bought it in London and your opinion is that it's the real thing.'

'The mask?' Blake sounded surprised. 'Do you think that has something to do with this?'

'I'm almost certain that it's central to everything that's happening. If Simon hadn't been in this state I'd have brought it with us, just to prevent it falling into Caltro's hands. Right now, I think we have to make sure it's as far away from Simon. These things have been known to bring curses with them, anything which belonged to these superstitious people and associated with their kings or religion.'

'Like those things which were brought out of the tomb of Tutankhamen, you mean?'

'Something like that, only in this case even more so. I've had dealings with these witchdoctors before and although some of their spells and incantations may be ascribed to self-induced hypnosis on the part of the victim, I saw enough to convince me that there's a lot more to it than we realize.'

'Simon never spoke of it when I visited him last. I only knew about it when he mentioned it in his letter. Either he didn't have it when I came or, for some reason, he didn't want me to examine it.'

'So you've never seen it before?'

'Not before tonight.'

'That's strange. We'd better question

him as soon as he's in a condition to talk. I think there are quite a lot of things Simon will have to explain in the very near future if we're to help him at all.'

'What do we do if Caltro decides to come after him? He's bound to find out sooner or later what we've done and if Simon is as important to him as you seem to think he is, won't he try to get him back?'

'I'm quite sure he will. We'll have to be on our guard night and day. We mustn't let Simon out of our sight for a single instant.'

Nayland drove carefully through the chill darkness. There were more clouds now, pressing in from the horizon, blotting out the white face of the moon for long moments at a time, making it difficult to see the road.

There were a hundred burning questions running through his mind, demanding answers. What if Caltro already knew what they had done and already had his own flat under observation? From past experience, he knew that the people had their own means of obtaining information and some of these methods were, at the moment, beyond the explanations of science.

He had the distinct impression that Caltro wanted that mask for his own purposes.

He cut a corner dangerously close and forced his mind back to the present. The questions would have to remain unanswered for a little while. Maybe, he thought, Simon knew most of the answers, but he wouldn't be in any condition to talk for some time yet.

A few moments later, he guided the car in to the side. The house was in darkness, but it was obvious that Sims, the manservant, had heard them arrive, for within seconds a light flashed on in one of the lower windows and the door opened as he got out of the car and stood stretching himself for an instant.

'Mr. Nayland, sir. Is anything wrong?'

Sims, stockily-built, balding a little with a fringe of grey hair around his temples, came hurrying towards them.

'Nothing to worry about, Sims,' said Nayland quietly.

The manservant glanced down at the

still body in the back of the car.

'Why, it's Mr. Merrivale. Has he met with an accident, sir?'

'Yes, in a way. I want you to bring some warm blankets and some hot water. Quickly.'

'Very good, sir.' Sims recovered his composure almost immediately and hurried off into the house, leaving the door wide open for them to carry the inert body of Simon Merrivale inside.

'Put him on the couch over there,' muttered Nayland, breathing heavily. 'I'll be able to tell how bad he is once I examine him in the light.'

Blake stood up and shrugged his powerful shoulders. 'He still seems to be unconscious. No sign of him coming round at all.'

'Sometimes they remain like this for days. If they really did go through with the Black Mass, then we may never rouse him. Caltro will be the only man who could do that.'

For a moment, the two men stared at each other in silence, then back down again at the still body on the couch.

Simon Merrivale's eyes were half-closed and there was an expression on his face such as neither of them had ever seen before.

A look in which fear and terror and something more were all blended into something that was unutterably horrible.

Sims came hurrying in at that moment with blankets and a jug of hot water. He stood by with a helpless look on his features as Nayland wrapped the blankets carefully around Merrivale's body. Finally, he stood up.

'Better get us both a drink, Sims,' he said tersely, 'We need one after what we've been through.'

'Very good, sir.' The manservant went out of the room without asking any further questions.

'You've got a damned good man there,' remarked Blake.

The other nodded. 'He's one of the best. Never asks questions no matter what time of the morning I arrive or how peculiar things may seem.'

Sims came back a moment later with the drinks. 'Straight bourbon, sir,' he said quietly. Nayland took his and sipped it appreciatively. The raw spirit went down into his stomach and stayed there, bringing some of the warmth and feeling back into his body.

Now that the nightmare in his mind had receded a little and they were away from that place with its crude altar and weird cabalistic designs inlaid in the floor, he was feeling a little better, a little more able to think clearly again.

He still wasn't sure exactly how they were going to go about getting Simon out of Caltro's clutches and bring him back to normal. So far, it seemed, the victory lay with them. They might have difficulty in rousing the other from his trance-like state, but so long as they managed to keep him where Caltro couldn't reach him, he felt that half the battle had been won.

He was suddenly aware that Sims was standing hesitantly in the background, looking down at him uncertainly.

'Yes, Sims?'

'I was just wondering, sir. Did you wish me to do anything with this?'

'What is it, Sims?'

The other brought something out into the light and Nayland felt a little thrill of horror run through him. He realized what it was. The feathered headdress and mask that, as far as he remembered, they had left behind them in Merrivale's hallway.

'Where the devil did you get that?' he demanded.

Sims looked momentarily surprised at his tone, then said evenly: 'I found it in the back of the car, sir. I thought it was something important; one of Mr. Merrivale's trophies, perhaps, which you'd brought back with you.'

Nayland felt his gaze drawn hypnotically towards the thing in the other's hands.

Beside him, Blake got to his feet, his chair clattering to the floor behind him.

'How in God's name did that thing get there? I'll swear that it wasn't in the car a few moments ago when I got out. We'd have noticed it if it had been.'

Nayland tried to think, to remember. Strange disconnected images were running through his mind and it was difficult to relate them properly.

'There has to be some explanation for it,' he said eventually. 'The thing didn't just get in there by itself.' He turned to the manservant. 'Just leave it there, Sims. We'll put it away in a safe place until Mr. Merrivale is well enough to take it back with him.'

'Yes, sir.'

When the manservant had withdrawn. Nayland turned to his companion. 'I don't want to frighten you by telling you this, Richard,' he said slowly, choosing his words carefully, 'but I think you ought to know the position as far as I've been able to ascertain it.

'I'm quite sure I was right when I suggested they intended performing the ceremony of the Black Mass, with Simon as the central figure. The fact that yesterday was his birthday was more than a mere coincidence. There are times when all events are favourable to their diabolical plans, when the evil ones take a human form for themselves, control it completely, so that they may use it to compete with the good.'

70

'And you think that Simon is — '

'No, not completely, thank God.' The other shook his head. 'Although I've a strong suspicion that if we hadn't burst in on them earlier in the evening, they would have gone through with their plans and we would have been unable to save him.'

'Then this — ' Blake hesitated before inclining his head towards Merrivale's body on the couch.

'This, I think, is some state of shock brought on by some experience he's been through. I'm fairly certain of that now. Whatever they did to him, it doesn't seem likely they forced him to cross the abyss. He isn't one of them yet, if that's what you mean.'

'But he's dabbled in this sorcery?'

Nayland nodded. 'I'm afraid that's true. They have some kind of hold over him. Blackmail, perhaps. They usually succeed in finding out something about their victims. After all, none of us is perfect and they can use whatever knowledge they have to force people into their circle.

'Then they promise them all the power under the sun, riches beyond all their dreams, everything they can wish. And that's usually a sufficiently good inducement for their victims to remain in the circle, particularly after they've seen a little of what these people can do.'

'They won't like it then once they discover we've taken Simon from them.' Blake uttered a harsh laugh but there was no mirth in it.

'Exactly. One of us must remain with Simon every single minute. That's vitally important. We'll take turns through the night. I'll take the first two hours and you the next. If anything happens while either of us is watching we must wake the other without delay. There's another couch here, so we'll sleep on that so as to be within easy call.'

Blake nodded. Getting to his feet, Nayland rang for the servant.

'Yes, sir?' Sims stood in the doorway, his face expressionless.

'We've decided to take turns sleeping down here, Sims. Bring a couple of blankets for us, will you?'

'Certainly, sir.'

'I don't think they'll try anything tonight,' Nayland said after the other had gone, trying to force conviction and evenness into his tone. 'But if they do, we've got to be ready for them. My only fear is that they know Simon's here and they decide to hit us before we can prepare ourselves.'

'What sort of thing do you expect?'

Nayland bit his lip. 'That depends on how much they want him back. They may try to break in and take him by force, but from what I've learned about Caltro, I think he'll try something more subtle than that. He may try to call Simon away. He'll snap out of the trance quite suddenly, unexpectedly, before we're aware of it and try to get away. If that happens, we may have to strap him to the couch.'

He saw Blake's eyes widen in surprise. Evidently this was all new to him and strangely fantastic. He could see that the other only half-believed what he was hearing. Strong-arm men breaking in by force, he could imagine, but intangible forces acting in strange ways across distance, was almost beyond Blake's comprehension.

'There's one other thing I don't quite understand. Is it Simon Caltro really wants or this mask?'

Rubbing his chin, Nayland considered the other's question for a few moments before replying. 'I think he wants both. He clearly believes the mask is a highly potent force for evil and it's almost certain he's made a comprehensive study of the ancient African tribes, their religions, and the powers the witchdoctors possessed. It's equally likely he's been looking for this relic for some considerable time but unfortunately Merrivale got his hands on it first.'

Blake looked puzzled. 'Then why doesn't he just take it, especially now that Merrivale is clearly under his influence?'

Nayland gave a grim smile. 'The fact is that with these ancient evil objects, he can't just take it or force Merrivale to give it to him. *Merrivale must give it to him of his own free will.*'

'I think I understand what you're

saying but he still wants our friend back. Just how will he do that? Bring some of his friends and break down the door?'

'Those are the usual things,' Nayland explained. 'If they fail, believe me, they have some more terrible and frightening things in store for us. They may send a messenger to fetch him. What form this messenger will take, I don't know. But if that happens, then there may be nothing we can do, seeing that we've had no opportunity to prepare ourselves.'

Blake opened his mouth to ask more questions, but at that moment, Sims returned with the blankets. He placed them down on the spare couch then straightened: 'Will there be anything else, sir?'

'No, that will be all for tonight, Sims. Better get some sleep. Sorry to have kept you up so late.'

No sooner had the other closed the door behind him than Nayland walked swiftly across and locked it on the inside, slipping the key into his pocket.

'One fortunate thing about this room,' he said quietly, 'is that it has only the one door and one window. There are no other entrances, or exits.'

Blake nodded, then walked over to the empty couch and took off his jacket, draping it over the back of a chair. With an effort, he stifled a yawn. 'I never realized I was letting myself in for anything like this when I got in touch with you,' he said hoarsely.

'You'd better get some sleep too,' said Nayland. 'I'll wake you in two hours' time.'

Within minutes, the other was asleep and Stephen Nayland leaned back in his chair, feeling the tenseness begin to grow in his brain as silence returned to the house.

Try as he would, he found it impossible to get the memory of that terrible figure, wearing the grotesque mask which had passed them on the stairs of Merrivale's house, out of his mind.

What the devil had that been? It couldn't have been a figment of his own overwrought imagination because Blake had seen it too and he had never heard of two people having the same illusion at the same time, unless both were under mass hypnosis, which hadn't been possible at the time.

No, he thought savagely, there had to be some other explanation, although at the moment, he found it impossible to find one. And the fact that the native they had seen looking for all the world like one of the witchdoctors of the African jungles, had also possessed a strange resemblance to Merrivale, made it all the more frightening and disconcerting.

With an effort, he forced steadiness into his mind and body. There was no sense in panic at a time like this, he decided. That wouldn't help and if anything really happened, he would need all of his wits about him if he were to defeat this terrible evil that seemed to be hanging over them.

5

The Messenger!

As he sat there, the stillness and the emptiness of the house began to settle around him more and more. There was still the wind outside, at first very low and quiet and then suddenly shriller as it began to stir restlessly around the walls. Murmuring voices seemed to rise and fall with the wind and, acting on a sudden impulse, he got to his feet and switched off the light.

The curtains over the window had been drawn aside and with the light on, it was impossible to see what was happening outside. It took all of his nerve to force himself to sit there and only the comforting thought that Blake was lying asleep less than three feet away kept him in his seat.

Gradually, his eyes became accustomed to the darkness. There was a faint shimmering of moonlight outside and the tree close by the window threw a weird pattern of light and shadow over the floor.

He began to wish that he didn't feel so jumpy. Maybe, he reasoned, he had made a mistake in switching off the light. If there was one thing these creatures didn't like, it was the light. They were nocturnal things, preferring the darkness and the shadows that seemed to be their natural home.

He managed a wry grin in the darkness. After all, it wasn't likely they would try anything tonight. His mind was thinking clearly now. But where had he heard all that before? He mustn't let his mind lull him into a false state of security.

His brain rambled on, fitting facts together, trying to make sense out of all that had happened since he had landed in London. How long had Merrivale been mixed up in this terrible business? In spite of the fact that he had tried to keep some of the seriousness of the situation from Blake, he still felt worried. Merrivale seemed to be in a state of deep coma.

There were only two possibilities as far as he could see.

Either the horror of what had happened earlier that evening after they had left him in the hands of Caltro had so shocked his brain that it had retreated into some insulated, unfeeling part of his mind, or they had really taken some degree of control over him and, to a certain extent, he was already in their power.

Black Magic had been practised under Merrivale's roof not once, but many times, in the past. He felt sure of that. But just how far they had gone during those ceremonies, he wasn't quite sure.

He glanced down at his watch, holding it close to his face so that he could just make out the luminous hands.

It was a little after one-thirty. Everything was quiet and still and ominous.

In his ears was the low moan of the wind, rising, sighing out of the yellow, liquid moonlight through a small gap in the curtains. They suddenly billowed out into the room, spreading outwards like a pair of clutching hands, reaching towards him in the dimness.

The curtain cord began to hammer feebly against the glass of the window, swaying slightly with the wind. He endured it for as long as he could, then crossed over to the window and tied the cord back against the wall.

This done, he half-turned to go back to his seat when something caught his attention, something moving with a peculiarly sinuous motion at the corner of his vision.

He grew aware that his fingers were gripping the ledge of the window with a savage intensity. The thing came nearer, moving through the trees that bordered the street and he knew with a sudden conviction, that it was nothing even remotely human.

His mind was beginning to race and reel inside his head. The red blood was pounding incessantly in his veins. The black shadow continued to flow forward with an avid, hungry motion. With a sudden movement, he stepped back into the room.

He tried to see it clearly, but it was

impossible. The moonlight appeared to flow around it, altering the outline in some strange way that didn't make sense. Something with arms and legs but that was all he could clearly see.

Cold sweat trickled down his taut face. It was as if he were suffocating and his life depended on him getting out of that room immediately. With a supreme effort, he pulled himself together and forced himself to think clearly and coherently.

Even as he pulled back into the room and touched Blake on the shoulder to wake him, Simon Merrivale mumbled something hoarsely under his breath and tried to sit up, his eyes staring wildly at something in front of him as though seeing someone inside the room.

Blake was awake in an instant. He swung his feet to the floor and sat for a brief instant, looking about him into the darkness.

'What is it, Stephen? Something wrong?'

'I'm afraid so. Now listen carefully because there isn't much time for me to explain. What I feared has happened. Caltro knows what we've done and he's guessed that we have Simon here. He's now going to do his damnedest to get him away from us and we've got to stop him at all costs.'

'You can rely on me, Stephen.'

'Good. There's something outside, coming closer to the window. Whatever it is, you can be sure that it's evil. If only we had a piece of the Sacred Host with us we'd stand a good chance. It would be our best protection against these things.

'As it is, we'll have to make do with what we have. I hope you know how to pray because that's going to be our only standby now.'

Something rattled against the window-pane, but Nayland didn't look round. The immediate danger, he reasoned, would not come from that direction. It would come from Simon Merrivale himself.

A moment later, Merrivale pushed himself upright from the couch and staggered forward across the room, moving towards the door. His gaze seemed fixed on something directly ahead of him and one arm was outstretched as though to fend off something horrible which was beckoning him forward.

'Take care that he doesn't make a run for the window as soon as he discovers that the door is locked and bolted,' warned Nayland.

Merrivale twisted the handle of the door, experimentally at first; then more savagely until, realizing that it was useless, he turned back into the middle of the room to face them.

'Oh God, what an expression,' muttered Blake.

'He can't see us,' said Nayland quietly. 'He's acting under their compulsion. He knows nothing of what's going on around him. All he knows is that he has to get out of here and back to Caltro.'

Quite suddenly, Merrivale lunged across the room with an unexpected rapidity, but Nayland recovered his wits instantly and jumped after him, catching him around the ankles and pulling him to the floor.

'Here, help me to hold him down,' he gasped.

After a brief struggle, they succeeded in pinning the other to the floor, his arms pinioned, his head forced well back. Even then, Merrivale did not cease to struggle. Strange, animal sounds came from his quivering lips. His throat muscles moved incessantly and his chest heaved.

'This isn't going to be easy,' muttered Nayland. 'I think you'd better put the light on. It might help us.'

Blake got to his feet and stumbled across the room, cursing a little as he knocked into the furniture in the darkness. Out of the corner of his eye, Nayland saw the dark shape that suddenly appeared outside the window, looking in at them with a malevolent leer on its face. Two eyes, red with hatred, stared back at him and there seemed to be twin flames leaping at the back of them, boring into his very soul.

There was something empty and chill and dead about the way that thing had come forward, gliding with that oddly sinuous motion. And there was something decidedly ugly and evil in the way it came forward against the window with an obvious purpose, a singleness of design.

The next minute, Blake had snapped on the light and the thing was no longer there. It seemed to have melted away into the shadows as though it had never existed. But Nayland knew that it was still out there, biding its time, waiting for its opportunity to enter the room and take what it had come for.

He felt suddenly dry-throated and got slowly to his feet, trying to breathe slowly.

'That's better,' he said weakly. 'They nearly took us by surprise.'

'How's Simon?'

The other glanced down. Merrivale had relapsed into his original comatose state, his lips twisted back over his teeth in an animal snarl that did something terrible to his face. His eyes were wide open, staring at the ceiling over his head, fixed, but unseeing.

'What do you think of him?' asked Blake suddenly.

'It's far more serious than I'd thought at first. They seem to have some control over him which we may find difficult to break.'

Going over to the small table, Nayland poured himself a drink from the crystal decanter. He felt the sweat popping out on his forehead although the air inside the room was cold. His throat was suddenly dry and stiff.

'Do you mean that he may be insane — that this state could be permanent?' There was incredulity in Blake's tone.

'I wouldn't say that he was insane by any means. He isn't.'

He shuddered and turned away from the twisted face. The old fear and the black nightmare were back again in his mind.

'I think he's coming round again,' said Blake suddenly.

Nayland looked down. Even as he watched, the other's features changed violently, convulsively. He twisted and writhed on the floor in his unnatural sleep. His lips drew back still tighter across his bared teeth and he snarled and groaned loudly.

Desperately, he tried to lift himself from the carpet. His face became distorted, the face of a fiend, which startled both of the men.

'God, what's wrong with him?' asked Blake. 'I've never seen anyone like this before.'

'I think there's a devil in him.' Nayland reached up and took the small golden crucifix from around his neck. 'This should tell us whether I'm right or not.'

He leaned further forward as the other stepped close to the struggling, figure of Simon Merrivale and laid the cross gently on his forehead.

'I think you'll see in a few moments. If I'm right — Ah, just as I feared.'

Merrivale twisted and moaned afresh in his coma. His eyes closed momentarily and then flicked wide open again, staring straight at them, but there was no sign of recognition.

Horror stared out of them. The lips were curled back in a snarl of almost bestial hatred. For an instant, Nayland had the unshakable impression that the teeth at the corners of the other's mouth lengthened, became pointed, until they were long and yellow like fangs.

Bending swiftly, he picked up the small crucifix and replaced it around his neck.

'Good God.' Blake went down on one knee, leaning closer. 'That mark on his forehead. What on earth could have caused that?'

Nayland stood quite still, looking down and shivering a little. The feeling of evil crystallized inside his mind and he suddenly remembered that thing outside in the moonlight.

'There is a devil in him,' he muttered thinly. 'That's the only explanation I have so far. It's been almost four years since I ever saw anything like this. But you don't believe in devils and demons, do you?'

'And what if I did?' Blake looked perplexed. 'Would it help me to understand that at all?'

'Perhaps, but — ' The rest of Nayland's sentence remained unsaid. The lights in the room suddenly dimmed and flickered unsteadily. Dark shadows at the corners of the room reached out towards the center and the air turned suddenly far colder than before.

Nayland felt sick in his stomach. Caltro had failed in his initial attempt to get Merrivale away from them. Now he was sending the messenger to take him away.

Images of the black things he had

encountered in the past kept trying to shape themselves in Nayland's overwrought imagination. He fought desperately to keep them out of his mind. He would need all of his wits about him during the next hour or so.

But if they could succeed in keeping them at bay until dawn, then they might still be safe.

'I must get out of here. I must get out of here!'

Nayland heard the words, but failed to realize for the moment who had uttered them. At first, he thought it was Merrivale and a moment fled before he recognized Blake's plaintive voice, reaching him from the flickering dimness.

Almost before he was aware of it, Blake ran for the door and began twisting the handle insanely, babbling at the top of his voice.

Desperately, Nayland caught hold of him by the arm and pulled him round, forcing him to face him.

'Quiet!' he snapped loudly. Drawing back his arm, he hit the other hard across the face with the back of his hand, hoping to evoke a shock response. For a moment, the other continued to mutter obscene words to himself, then the look of madness in his eyes died away and sanity returned.

'What happened?' he asked weakly.

'They tried to take control of you,' said Nayland grimly, 'to divert our attention from Merrivale. From now on, if you feel anything trying to reach into your mind start to pray. Anything you like, but keep on praying, you understand?'

The other nodded slowly and wiped the sweat from his forehead with the back of his hand. 'I think so,' he murmured weakly. He followed Nayland back into the middle of the room where Simon still lay on the carpet, his fingers clenching and unclenching by his sides.

The light gave a final flicker and then winked out, leaving them in almost complete darkness. Nayland turned his head slowly. Some moonlight flooded in through the window, but it seemed to give very little light and the shadows inside the room suddenly assumed alarming proportions and terrifying shapes that twisted and cavorted around their feet like living things.

Panic thoughts chased themselves through Nayland's mind as he stood there, fingering the crucifix around his neck. If the worst came to the worst, it was their only protection and God alone knew how potent it would be against the evil that surrounded them.

He turned his head swiftly. Was that something moving over there by the door? Whether it was or not, a fresh spasm of fear swept over him. Dimly, he was aware of a clock chiming the hour in the distance and then, quite suddenly, all noise seemed to stop. Cold sweat broke out on his body.

The thing that had been Merrivale, lying on the floor at their feet, suddenly got up and stood facing them, a tall yet slightly hunched creature out of the worst of their nightmares.

It wore the mask and headdress that had been lying on the floor near the couch and there was now no doubting the fact that this was no longer Merrivale, but someone else, something exuding an indefinable aura of evil.

Nayland's conscious mind was hammering away at him: *This isn't real. It isn't real. It won't hurt you, because it's only part of your imagination. Don't look at it because you're becoming hypnotized. Break the spell. Look away — anywhere!*

With an effort, he dragged his eyes away from it.

Another dark shadow appeared at the window, peering in. Nayland caught a fragmentary glimpse of liquid moonlight on a face rotten with corruption, a nightmare creature with dead unblinking eyes that stared right through him. A creature of hell, conjured up by these people to overcome them and take Simon Merrivale back to their ranks.

He knew that his mind was slowly disintegrating. That it was gradually going to pieces under the terrible strain and when that terrible horror got into the room, he knew that it was possible he would go screaming mad.

He had the impression that Blake was beginning to scream noiselessly deep down in his throat. His lips were trembling violently and his hands were shaking, reaching for his throat.

Madly, he tried to pray but the words refused to come. The creature outside was beating on the windowpane now, hammering at the thin, fragile glass with taloned, bony fingers. His raving mind told him that it was only a matter of time before it was in the room with them.

For a moment, he had forgotten about Merrivale, or the thing that had once been him. Now, in his place, stood this apparition that could only have a place in the depths of the African jungles. A shaman, a witchdoctor, somehow possessing Simon Merrivale's body, taking over his mind, moving his limbs until they responded to this alien will.

The air in the room was a thick, almost liquid substance, intensely cold, and with a pungent smell that cloyed the back of his nostrils, making him feel sick inside. A tremor passed over him. The thing with the hideous mask was coming towards them, casting an aura of evil before it.

Blake was screaming thinly at the top

of his voice, gibbering strange words that made little sense as he tried to pray and the words came out all wrong. Whatever it was, the creature seemed awfully sure of itself, moving forward with a firm tread, hands reaching out towards him, ready to clutch and grip.

If it breathed, he could not hear it as it shambled forward, hunched up, the moonlight glistening a little on the half-naked body. The eyes seemed to be gazing past him and yet he knew that they were not; in reality the thing's whole attention was on him. Almost as though it knew that whatever it had to fear, it would come from him and not Blake.

But it did not seem to be an intelligent attention that was fixed upon him. He had the horrified impression that it was the unreflecting, unthinking attention of someone who does not think but trusts to a higher power to do all the thinking for him.

The mask was a truly hideous creation. The feathers of the plumed headdress ruffled a little as though a wind had caught them, but there was no wind in the room. He threw a swift glance towards the windows, and his mind went suddenly blank as he saw that they were already half-open and the thing outside was climbing into the room.

Hell glared redly out of its slitted eyes. This, he thought with what was left of his failing mind, was the evil messenger which Caltro had sent. Fear was a loud voice shouting inside his brain. Madly, he plucked the crucifix from around his neck and held it out in front of him, raising it high above his head. He felt something thrusting down against his arm, trying to push it down against his side and there seemed to be some malevolent force reaching out from the darkness near the window, trying to drown out the faintly glittering light of the crucifix in his trembling fingers.

Desperately, his lips moved, shaping the words of the Lord's Prayer, but most of the words refused to come. Everything seemed to be jumbled up inside his head, making no sense at all.

Voices were murmuring against his ear. Chanting words that didn't make sense, although he had the impression that he had heard them somewhere before and ought to know their meaning.

He shook his head several times to clear it. There appeared to be a thin ray of brilliance emanating from the crucifix as he held it up and the crushing pressure eased a little. He could feel his nerves tautening, stretching themselves to breaking point. Almost, he thought, he could detect Caltro's harsh, ominous laughter hanging in the air over his head.

The stumbling, loathsome thing at the window suddenly uttered a harsh shriek of diabolical rage as the beam from the cross pulsed more strongly and struck it. The lights near the ceiling flickered again and began to increase in brilliance.

After a moment, he realized that he was praying softly and steadily under his breath, mouthing the words from shaking lips. He started sharply; then took a tight grip on his mind. He had the feeling that the creature near the window, filled with an eager, hungry evil, was fading slowly.

The impulse to turn and run for the door exploded within him and became an urge which he had to fight hard to control, but some latent protective sense combined with the fear of what would happen once he turned his back on these creatures, prompted him to stay there and face them squarely and let matters take their own course.

The thing remained there for the best part of five minutes as far as he could judge; then faded slowly away into smoke. The moonlight flooded into the room in the same instant that the lights came on fully; and when he looked down at his feet again, it was simply the body of Simon Merrivale that lay there, breathing heavily and harshly.

The mask and headdress lay on the floor near the couch where they had always been since Sims had laid them down. Madly, he sucked in a harsh, sobbing breath and felt the pressure in his chest ease a little. He remained perfectly still for several seconds, fighting to regain control of his raging emotions.

His whole body shook and tingled with that strangely terrifying palpitation which comes after a close escape from some dreadful disaster or after awaking from a terrible nightmare.

Blake sat slumped on the couch, his face buried in his hands. His body was shaking uncontrollably. Finally, he said haltingly:

'Hell, I never want to go through anything like that again. It was horrible!'

'I don't think they'll try again, not tonight anyway.' Nayland sat down beside him, allowing his entire body to go limp. It was as though all of the strength had been drained from him so that it would have been impossible for him to have stood upright even if he had wanted to.

'What about Simon?'

'I think he'll be all right in the morning. They've made their play and it's failed. If they decide to try again, they'll try something different the next time. By then, we'll be prepared for them.'

A shiver passed through him and he sat there for a long moment until he had full control of himself again. Then he stood up, went over to the small table and poured two glasses from the decanter. Handing one to Blake, he said thinly,

'Here, drink this, it'll bring back some of the life into your body.'

'Thanks.' The other nodded and drained his glass in a single gulp. 'I needed that.'

Nayland sipped his drink slowly. Out of the corner of his eye, the mask intruded upon his vision and he felt more strongly than ever before, that the key to most of the mystery lay with it, rather than with this man, Caltro. If only he knew the history of such a hideous relic.

6

The Voodoo Curse

It was almost nine o'clock the following morning when Nayland had the first of his visitors. By that time, Merrivale had been removed to one of the bedrooms upstairs and appeared to be sleeping soundly.

Blake had brought in two cups of black coffee a moment before Sims arrived in the doorway and announced: 'There's a — gentleman — says he'd like to have a word with you if it's convenient, sir.'

Nayland looked up in surprise. His first thought was that Caltro had decided to take matters into his own hands and had come in person in an attempt to get Merrivale back. But he dismissed the idea almost immediately. It was unlikely that the other would play into his hands in this way.

'Did he give his name, Sims?'

'No, sir. I'm afraid not. He merely said that you wouldn't know his name, but that what he has to say to you will be vitally important and will possibly have some bearing on certain events which may have happened during the past few days.'

'That's curious.' Nayland fingered his chin and looked puzzled. 'It certainly sounds as though he knows something of what's been happening although I've no idea who he can be.'

'He isn't — English, sir,' put in Sims quietly. 'He's an African.'

'An African! You mean a Negro?'

'Exactly, sir.'

Nayland nodded. 'I think you'd better show him in right away, Sims,' he said suddenly. He turned to Blake.

'This may be important. If he's come here for the reason I think he has, we may be one step further towards solving this devilish mystery.'

There was a sudden movement in the doorway. Nayland glanced up. The man who stood there, although dressed in modern European clothes, seemed ill at ease in them and Nayland had the impression that, even here, he would have looked more at home in the tribal costume of the men of the African interior.

He was tall for a native, with a cultured, intelligent face but his eyes had a purpose more important merely than looking and seeing. Except to a person of considerable self-assurance, they could have been intolerable whenever he chose to make them so.

At the moment, however, they were amiable but filled with an expression of worried anxiety.

'Mr. Nayland?' he said hesitantly, stepping forward into the middle of the room.

'That's right,' Nayland said slowly. 'I understand you wanted to see me about something important.'

The man seemed to draw back like a well-trained leopard and Nayland felt a strange, unaccountable shiver course through him as he remembered the men he had seen before in the dark jungles. Men who became animals at the night of the full moon, took on the hideous shape that slid through the undergrowth among the black shadows after their victims, ripping and clawing and murdering.

'I tried to get in touch with a man called Merrivale,' explained the other, sitting in the chair that Nayland indicated, 'but unfortunately, that was impossible. I attempted to see him several times during the past few weeks, but always I was told that he was not at home to callers. Once, I met a man named Caltro there and then I knew why he wouldn't see me.'

'At the moment, although Mr. Merrivale is here in this house, I'm still afraid you won't be able to see him. But if there is anything we can do to help you — '

'I think I understand,' said the other slowly. 'I have had the feeling that he is in great danger from these people but it would seem he has a will of his own and does not take too kindly to advice, even that which is well-meaning. Perhaps he does not know the terrible power of the forces he is dealing with.'

'Perhaps,' interrupted Nayland impatiently, 'but supposing you tell us where you fit into this mystery.'

'I have come here all the way from Africa to take back something of great value which was stolen from my tribe. It must be returned to them or terrible evil will follow in its wake. I beg of you to help me to find it.'

'And what makes you think I have it?'

'Because I don't think you can help it. You have Mr. Merrivale here. Then I am sure that the mask and headdress of Shabaka, the greatest of our witchdoctors is with you. Tell me, Mr Nayland,' he leaned forward and his voice dropped to an almost confidential whisper: 'Has anything strange happened while that headdress and mask have been in his possession?'

'Some things have occurred — yes,' admitted Nayland. 'Are you trying to tell us that these are to be attributed to something supernatural connected with these things?'

'Ah, so you have seen something.' There was a note of triumph in the other's voice. 'It is as the Council prophesied before they sent me, Chalka, to bring back the sacred mask and headdress.'

'We saw something that, so far, we haven't been able to explain,' interrupted Blake, stirring uneasily in his chair.

'But you are still skeptical,' observed the other. 'Mr. — ?'

'Blake. Just let's say that I have a scientific mind.'

'I rather think that you'll find some things in this world which cannot be answered by science, Mr. Blake.'

'Are we to understand that you know what this thing can do?'

Before their visitor could reply, Nayland asked tersely, 'Before you answer that, I'd like to ask you how you've managed to trace Mr. Merrivale. At the moment, the only suggestion I can make is that you're part of this cult yourself, hoping to get it back for this man Caltro. You say your tribal council asked you to find it and take it back to Africa but we've no proof of that.'

The other spread his hands in a gesture of resignation. 'What proof can I give you? I know nothing of this man Caltro. It took me over a year to discover that it had been sold to the owner of a shop in

London. I offered to buy it from him but the price he asked was far more than any money I had. I tried to get more but when I returned he told me it had been bought by a man named Merrivale. It was not too difficult to find him through the telephone directory.'

The native looked at each of them with a disconcerting gaze. 'But in answer to your question, Mr. Blake, I think I ought to begin at the very beginning,' he went on, 'and then perhaps you will be able to see why it is so important that I take these sacred relics back to my tribe. Only then will the curse cease.

'There are certain legends of my tribe connected with the mask and headdress. They tell of a time when Shabaka was alive, the most powerful witchdoctor in the country. Some say that he traded with the Evil Ones to gain the knowledge for his spells, none of which could be broken. When he was killed, by treachery, he laid a curse on his mask and headdress. A voodoo, if you like.

'You see,' he went on, 'I have lived among my people for most of my life, except for five years which I spent in this country. I learned many things here, but nothing to explain the things I have seen back in the jungle.'

'I, too, have seen strange things in the jungle,' said Nayland. 'I'm inclined to believe what you've told us. If you could only tell us just what these curses are and how we may be able to counter them . . . '

The native looked across at him without smiling.

'When the moon is full, anyone coming into contact with the mask and headdress becomes transformed into Shabaka. Some believe that he actually lives again, projecting his mind and body into that of his victim, awaiting his time to wreak vengeance on those who destroyed him. But now these relics are in England, a long way from my village. Nothing can stand against him while he occupies the body of one of his victims. And the spell cannot be broken until these sacred relics are returned to my tribe.

'Unfortunately, while here, he has met an evil power which may be greater than his own. He must kill me before I can return these artifacts. The sacred shrine in my village has only been used for good since he was destroyed. He knows the mask and headdress can be destroyed if they are simply placed upon it by the present witchdoctor. Whether he seeks this man Caltro, of whom I have heard a little, as an ally, or will try to kill him, I do not know. But he will use any means to gain possession of this black magic which Caltro has.'

'But that's impossible. A man who's been dead for so many years coming alive again.' Blake uttered a harsh laugh but there was no humour in it.

'No, Richard, not impossible,' said Nayland gently. 'It's we who are impossible. Impossible because we still retain our inflexible outlook on these supernatural phenomena, refusing to see further than those things our scientific instruments can measure and see and weigh.

'But there are other things in this world that we can't see or measure. The mysteries of the occult for example. You know, the occult is the biggest, damnedest slice of midnight blackness there is. It's there all the time, watching and waiting, altering and touching us in subtle ways that we don't recognize. Or if we do, we never believe them.

'I'm remembering now what we saw last night just before we discovered Merrivale in the hallway at his home — that creature which came out of the room at the top of the stairs and vanished at the bottom. That must have been this witchdoctor, Shabaka, in Merrivale's body, horribly transplanted there by the curse on these things.'

'You mean this curse could affect these things even after all this time?' asked Blake dubiously.

'I think some of the records have shown that destructive forces from that mysterious 'other side' have persisted for hundreds of years. There are numerous instances in the records, most of them well-authenticated.'

'And you think we've run up against one of them in this voodoo?'

'Exactly. I'm inclined to believe Chalka's story. Especially after what we saw last night.' Nayland turned to the native. 'One thing you haven't told us. Africa is a big place. Exactly where is your village?'

'I live in a small village called Obondo. It is situated more than two hundred miles from the coast.'

Nayland shrugged. 'I never heard of it.'

'Perhaps if you have a large-scale map of Africa I can show you.'

Pointing towards the bookcase, Nayland said, 'You'll find one there, Richard.'

Returning a few minutes later, Blake placed the map on the table. Chalka studied it intently for a full minute, then said: 'It is not marked here but nevertheless I can assure you it exists. I'll show you exactly where it is.' Taking the pen that Nayland handed to him, he marked a small cross on the map before straightening up.

'Then if you have the headdress here, perhaps you would return it to me and there will be no more curses on anyone unfortunate enough to come into contact with it,' said Chalka.

Nayland shifted uncomfortably in his seat. Indecision was strong within him. What the other had said had possessed a ring of truth, but the relics did not belong to him and he hardly felt justified in handing them over like this. This was something that required earnest consideration. He paused as another thought struck him. There was just the possibility that this was another trick employed by Caltro to get Merrivale back into his power again.

What if this man wasn't who he said he was? It was quite feasible that he was someone working for Caltro, probably someone from the Inner Circle itself, wanting to use the mask for their own evil purposes.

So he gave it to Chalka all trusting and once they had it in their possession, they would use it to destroy Simon's mind completely and then there would be no escape for him.

'I'll have to speak to Mr. Merrivale first,' he said, hedging. 'But I'm sure that once I've explained the position to him, he'll be only too glad to co-operate. If you could come back here this evening some time, about nine o'clock?'

The other got to his feet. There was a

strange look on his face but he merely said gravely: 'Very well; at nine o'clock. But I earnestly implore you not to be foolish and try to dabble in things that are best left alone. If this force is liberated, it can be a terrible thing. Death can come in many horrible ways. Mr. Nayland.'

Stephen wasn't sure whether that last remark about death had been intended as a warning or a threat. There was nothing on the other's face to indicate which it had been.

He waited until Chalka had left, then returned to the living room. Blake looked at him with an expression of mild surprise on his face.

'What on earth was all that rot about asking Simon?' he asked. 'You know damned well that he won't be in any condition to make decisions for God knows how long.'

'Precisely. But there's one important point that I'd almost overlooked.'

'Oh, what's that?'

'We've only got Chalka's word for it that he's come here directly from Africa to take this mask back to his tribe. It's more likely that he's been sent by Caltro to get the mask by trickery. I'm not sure whether these people realize the power of these relics, but once they do they won't rest until they've laid their hands on them. That could have been the first attempt.

'I needed time to think about this, that's why I put him off until tonight with that phony tale. I've got a feeling that something's going to break before long and when it does, it might give us a clue to who this man, Chalka, really is. If he's the genuine article, then we'll do everything we can to get these things back to him. If he isn't then we've lost nothing.'

★ ★ ★

The little thought that had been running lazily through Nayland's mind as he changed, suddenly came out into the open. What was Caltro up to now? It was difficult to believe that he would be remaining idle, although it was possible that the black, evil power that these creatures possessed was less active during the day.

The knowledge steadied him. Drying his hands and face, he slipped on his tie, knotted it quickly, and put on his jacket. It was with a feeling of satisfaction that he noticed that his hands were no longer shaking.

Blake was still in the dining room when he entered. In spite of the grin that the other gave him, he was surprised to find that he couldn't quite throw off the feeling of apprehensive fear that had descended upon him ever since the visit of Chalka almost an hour earlier.

'Somehow, things are turning out a little differently from what I expected,' he said quietly, closing the door behind him.

'You think they'll try again?'

'I'm sure they will. The question is, when and where.'

He glanced about him, his senses alert. He had the most uncertain feeling about the rooms that lay on the other side of that closed door through which he had just entered. He had felt that the moment he had stepped into this room, somebody had been out there, watching him, even though he had seen nothing.

He threw a swift, suspicious glance at the windows, expecting to see someone standing there. He saw nothing but the cool sunlight and the mist rising from the gardens.

Angrily he told himself that he was behaving like a stupid fool, scaring himself half to death when there was nothing, as yet, of which to be afraid.

He walked over to the window, aware that Blake's gaze was on him, watching him curiously. And he had the feeling that there were other eyes watching him from outside He glanced up and down the street, but there was no one there, although he had the unshakable impression that someone — or something — had stood there, on the pavement a bare instant before, and then melted away into the sunlight as though anticipating his motion.

He tried hard to throw off the feeling that he was being watched, that stealthy eyes were peering at him from outside — a quiet, faintly-audible breathing that he couldn't hear with his ears. Rather it was something he could just sense with his mind. His inner mind seemed to reach out of its own accord, out beyond the glass windows, into the sunlight, and seemed to detect a quiet, evil presence there.

Then he looked round sharply, directly across the garden and saw the tall, broadly-built figure watching him out of amused, slightly malevolent eyes.

Caltro!

He realized that Blake was looking at him queerly from further inside the room.

'Is there anything wrong, Stephen?'

'Caltro. He's outside. It looks as though he's decided to pay us a visit in person after all.'

'Caltro!' Blake walked quickly over to the window and looked out. 'What the devil can he want?'

'It's ten-to-one that he'll try to get Simon away under some pretext or another. One thing you must remember. Under no circumstances must we offer him anything to eat or drink. He can do little so long as we remember that.'

117

Blake nodded. 'I'm not sure that I understand why,' he said hurriedly. 'But you ought to know best.'

He glanced round sharply as Sims entered. There was a strange look on the manservant's face. He licked his lips nervously, then said thinly: 'There's a Mr Caltro waiting to see you, sir. He says that you are expecting him.'

'Show him in, Sims,' Nayland said, keeping his voice steady with an effort.

'Yes, sir.'

A moment later, the tall, fleshy figure of Caltro stood in the doorway looking across at them. There was a sardonic smile on his lips and an expression at the back of his eyes as though the Devil himself was looking out at them.

7

Terror by Day

Nayland shuddered inwardly at the sight of the fat, smoothly-rounded cheeks and the small, narrowed eyes, slanted like those of an Oriental beneath almost non-existent brows. The huge, balding head seemed balanced precariously on top of a body, which, although grotesquely fat and corpulent, still seemed a little too small for it.

With a bobbing motion, Caltro came into the room and laid his hat carefully on a nearby chair. He seemed to be completely at his ease. Too damned sure of himself, thought Nayland wildly. Just what was the other up to coming here like this?

'I understand that you have a friend of mine staying here with you, Mr Nayland. May I ask how he is this morning?'

Was there a touch of hidden menace in

that thick oily voice?

'I'm glad to say that he's quite well,' Nayland said slowly. 'At the moment, however, he's sleeping so I'm afraid you won't be able to see him.'

'A pity.' The other gave a wave of his thick hand. It was a gesture full of meaning and was not lost on Nayland. 'I trust that he won't be indisposed for too long. To tell you the truth, I was quite concerned about him. He hasn't been his usual self lately, but I suppose you know that for yourselves.'

Going across the room, he lowered his heavy bulk into one of the chairs and sat facing them with a smooth smile on his broad features. Something unclean and evil seemed to spread out from him in all directions, as if death and terror had been his constant companions for all of his life.

Nayland said sharply: 'Just why did you come here in the first place, Mr Caltro? I'm quite sure it wasn't because you are so concerned with Simon Merrivale's health.'

'Oh, but I am. Very concerned. You see he happens to be a very good and close friend of mine. But I wonder if you know just how important his health is to me.'

'If you're referring to last night's little demonstration then we have realized it,' Nayland said thinly.

He sat down and faced the other. Out of the corner of his eye, he was aware of Blake, hovering indecisively in the background, his face set and fixed. Poor Blake, he thought tensely, he doesn't really know what all this is about. If he did, he probably wouldn't be standing there so quietly, listening to them arguing.

Caltro suddenly leaned back in his chair, placing the tips of his thick, stubby fingers together. He said softly: 'Let's not beat about the bush any longer, Mr Nayland. You know that it is absolutely essential that I should have Mr Merrivale returned to me. He is extremely important to the work I'm doing and the sooner you both realize that your puny efforts cannot avail against the forces I have at my command, the easier it will be. I'll admit that you went a long way towards thwarting me last night, but if you persist in your foolish attempts to fight me, you will both be destroyed — utterly. Do you understand that?'

For a moment Nayland had a sense of toppling perspective as the other seemed to grow hugely; a terrifying figure that looked across at him with fearful, blazing eyes.

Then his vision steadied. Everything became normal again and Caltro was smiling blandly at him.

'You'll never get him back,' interrupted Blake, 'even if I have to kill you to stop you.'

Nayland saw that the other had the heavy metal poker in his right hand, his arm upraised. There was an expression of savage anger on the younger man's face as he lunged forward to strike.

'Don't, you fool!'

Nayland had only time to shout the warning before Caltro, scarcely moving in his chair, made a queer sign in the air in front of him with the forefinger of his right hand. For an instant, Nayland seemed to see the outline of the design traced there in a circle of fire. His lips were moving slowly, shaping the words of some odious incantation.

To Nayland's startled gaze, Blake stopped in mid-stride, his arm still upraised, his features contorted with fury. Then something seemed to happen inside him. His legs sagged and swayed beneath him as though no longer able to bear his weight. He crumpled, toppling forward, knocking aside the small table as he fell to the floor.

Nayland started to his feet, then sank back as the other said silkily, 'Your friend will recover in a little while, Mr Nayland. He is merely a fool who doesn't know what he is doing or what he is up against. But I think that should be a sufficient demonstration of the powers I possess. Now, where is Simon Merrivale?'

'He's where you won't be able to lay your evil hands on him,' said Nayland feebly.

'I warn you,' hissed Caltro harshly. 'If you try to interrupt my work again, I shall be forced to eliminate you altogether.'

His right arm reached out towards Nayland, grabbed the sleeve of his jacket and clung to it. There didn't seem to be much strength in the thick, rubbery fingers but the other could scarcely repress a shudder of revulsion as they touched him.

'I don't intend to leave this house without Simon Merrivale. You realize that by interfering with my work, you've delivered both yourself and your friend into my hands entirely. If necessary, when the time is once again right, we may have three victims for the Great Master, instead of only one.'

His sudden high laugh of triumph sent madness blazing like a searing flame through Nayland's mind. God alone knew how many poor, ignorant wretches had been enslaved by these people, killed perhaps on that black altar, to appease some hideous Black Deity, butchered by this crazy High Priest of Evil.

He grew aware that Caltro was speaking again. 'Very soon now, we shall perform the sacrifice, The Great Master will receive his victims and I shall be made one with the Dark One. The Grand Ipsissimus! Then, everything will be mine. No one will be able to stand against me.'

He leaned forward in his chair, his eyes staring into Nayland's with an expression of feral hunger and eagerness.

Quite suddenly, his head seemed to lift from his body, to float slowly into the air all by itself, outlined against the grey dimness of the room. But the oily smile was still there and the small dark eyes that looked steadily into his, peered down into his very soul.

Caltro's voice reached him as from a tremendous distance and yet the words were clearly audible:

'You're a fool to try to pit your feeble strength against mine. Nothing can stand against me.'

Then there was a hollow emptiness all around Nayland. He could feel his strength and his courage evaporating away inside him like water in a vacuum.

There was a dreadful bleakness in his mind that refused to go away. His body felt suddenly unclean as though a multitude of foul things were crawling all over his skin. There was that dark shadow again, thicker and more substantial this time, leaping forward to overwhelm him with an added strength.. The room felt suddenly cold.

Give in, screamed the tiny voice of madness in his brain; *give in, because it's useless to fight against this evil terror!*

Madly, he tried to trace the shape of the Cross in the air in front of him, tried desperately to lift his right hand. But there seemed to be some hideous force pulling it down, clamping it rigidly to his side, Sweat popped out on his forehead with the terrible effort.

He tried to open his mouth to scream, to pray, but no words came out.

Then, almost before he was aware of it, blackness surged up out of the floor, from the walls and ceiling over his head. He went out with a dull thudding in his brain and the leering face of Caltro staring at him from the darkness.

For a second, he thought he heard a dull booming of wild, triumphant laughter in his ears. Then there was nothing for a very long time.

★ ★ ★

His first sensation was of lying on something soft and yielding; his second was of the bright light shining almost directly into his eyes, the glare probing redly through the lids even before he opened them involuntarily.

Weakly, he turned his head away from the light, and tried to sit up. Surprisingly, he was able to do so and as he levered himself onto one elbow, the first memory impressions began filtering back into his brain.

'You'll be as right as rain in a few moments, sir. Just lie still,' said a familiar voice.

He blinked his eyes several times, the blood rushing to his head, pounding behind his temples. He saw that Blake was still unconscious, slumped in an armchair opposite him. A moment later, he saw the stocky figure of Sims on the far side of the room, busily pouring something from the decanter. There was the welcome chink of glasses, then the manservant came back.

'Better drink this down, sir,' he said casually, as though nothing had happened.

'Thanks, Sims.' Nayland took a sip; then clasped his hands to his ringing head. 'My God, what happened?'

'I'm not quite sure, sir. I came in a few moments ago and found you lying here unconscious on the floor with Mr. Blake beside you. I lifted you onto chairs to make you more comfortable. Was it anything to do with Mr. Caltro, sir?'

'Caltro!' With an effort, Nayland pulled himself to his feet and stood swaying slightly for a moment until his head cleared.

'That's right. Caltro. He was here, wasn't he?'

'Why yes, sir.' Sims looked puzzled. 'I heard the front door slam almost an hour ago, and assumed it was him leaving, although I didn't actually see him.'

'An hour.' Nayland glanced down at his watch. It was a little after midday.

'But that's impossible.' He looked down at Blake who suddenly mumbled a low moan and sat up, his face twisted with agony.

'Hell, what hit me?' He rubbed the muscles at the nape of his neck gingerly. 'I don't remember anything since — ' He broke off. 'Where the devil's Caltro?'

'He's gone,' said Nayland thinly. 'And it's my guess he's taken Simon with him!'

Together, they ran up the wide stairway into the room where they had left Merrivale asleep. The room was empty. The bed had been slept in, and a few of the sheets lay tangled up on the floor.

'It looks as though they had to take him away by force,' observed Blake grimly.

'Probably he knows enough now to be able to guess what's in store for him,' explained Nayland. He felt suddenly cold and a bitter sensation of defeat overwhelmed him. It seemed now that nothing they could do would save Simon.

'Do you think there's any chance at all of finding him then, Simon?'

Nayland shrugged. 'They could have taken him anywhere, I suppose. They wouldn't want to run the risk of us bursting in on them the next time as we did last night.'

He felt suddenly cold inside. Caltro would never take the other back to his own house, even though everything there was ready for the sacrifice of the Black Mass; that would have been making things too easy for him to be found again.

No, they'd pick some nice secluded spot, possibly well away from the city.

The utter hopelessness of the situation hit him with the force of a physical blow. If only they had a clue to go on, but Caltro would have been far too clever for that. He reached a sudden decision.

'There's just the possibility that we may find something to help us at Simon's place,' he said sharply. 'After all, that's where they intended carrying out the ceremony in the first place. We'd better get over here right away.'

'Anything will be better than just sitting around here doing nothing,' Blake agreed, 'particularly with Simon in the hands of those fiends. God, why did he have to be such a fool as to get into this mess to begin with?'

'Who knows why anybody does it?' said Nayland as they made their way down the stairs and out into the street. 'Some do it for the spirit of adventure. Others because they don't believe that evil really exists and just want to dabble in it, thinking they can back out of it any time they wish. It's like a new toy to some of them, only this is one thing they can't discard and throw away when they're tired of it.'

A few minutes later, Nayland opened the door of his car and slid himself behind the wheel, slamming the door behind him.

Nayland drove the powerful car with a kind of reckless abandon, keeping his foot down hard on the accelerator, peering ahead into the curtain of pouring rain that seemed to open up momentarily to let them pass, to slide over them like a river of darkness, and then close in behind the speeding car as if trying to block their way of return.

Twenty minutes later, they came within sight of the tall, rambling house that stood a little way back from the main road, half-hidden behind a veritable barrage of trees, as though deliberately trying to hide itself away from prying eyes.

Nayland swung the car in through the tall iron gates. There was the sudden crunch of gravel beneath the tires. Blake leaned forward in his seat and peered through the windscreen and Nayland did likewise.

Even if Caltro had taken Simon to some hideout in the country, it was still possible that he had left someone behind to watch the place just in case they returned.

There was that foreign-looking man-servant, for example. He might still be around somewhere and Nayland had the suspicion that he could be a nasty customer if the occasion warranted it.

The mansion showed up clearly in the dim light and he saw it fully for the first time since he had arrived back in England. The previous night it had been all shadow and darkness with no detail showing.

Tall, twisted towers ripped at the stormy sky, clawing defiantly for the foaming clouds. The windows reflected some of the grey light, like a hundred hungry eyes, staring and vacant, watching their approach.

They drew up in front of the house

with a squeal of brakes, parking a little to one side, leaving the car out of sight to a casual observer behind the tall bushes. It was a purely reflex measure because there was no point in keeping their presence a secret any longer, thought Nayland savagely. If there was anyone there, they would have spotted them by now and would be preparing a warm reception for them.

Their only hope of discovering anything of real importance lay in the possibility that Caltro had left the place empty, not considering it necessary to guard the room with the black sacrificial altar.

Nayland climbed out of the car and stood in the rain, looking up at the tall, rambling façade of the house. 'No sign of anyone at home,' he said hollowly. 'Fortunately, I still have the key from last night.'

The lock turned easily and the door swung open in front of them. Cautiously they stepped inside.

The hallway was empty and did not appear to have been used since the previous night when they had carried the limp form of Simon Merrivale out of the house. The door at the end of the hallway lay half-open. Nayland went forward quietly with Blake at his heels. The death-glazed eyes of the animal heads stared down at them impassively from the walls.

Carefully, he thrust the door open and stepped through into the room beyond. This was the first time he had seen it in daylight. His first impression was one of utter blackness. Heavy black curtains had been draped around the walls and over the windows, blotting out every ray of light from outside and only the feeble light that streamed through the open door picked out any of the details.

There was the unmistakable feel of evil here, something terrible and tangible that flowed around them like a dark cloud. Nayland had the feeling he was slowly suffocating, unable to breathe properly in the strangely thick atmosphere.

Feeling along the wall just inside the door, his fingers encountered the light switch and he snapped it down with a faintly explosive sound. The lights came on slowly, chasing the shadows away.

At the far end of the room stood the long, low altar with the black pitch and sulphur candles in their delicately carved silver sticks. Behind the altar, dominating everything, was a vast wooden cross, entwined about which was the huge shape of a serpent crushing it in its constricting coils representing the triumph of Evil over Good — the Devil coming into his own. Nayland repressed a sudden shudder and looked about him carefully. A brightly jeweled knife lay on the smooth black stone of the altar and close by, a huge book bound in red and black leather, the pages yellowed and brittle with age.

'Everything's still here,' he said finally in a hushed whisper. 'All laid ready for the ceremony of the Black Mass.'

'But is there anything here which might give us a clue as to where they've taken Simon?' inquired Blake.

Nayland shook his head. 'It was only a hunch I was playing but one thing is certain. They mean to come back here some time in the future, maybe when all this has blown over and been forgotten, otherwise they would have taken most of these things with them.'

'If only we could — '

'Quiet!' Nayland hissed the warning suddenly. He strained his ears to pick out the faintest sound. A moment later, he heard it again. It was the sound of footsteps on the gravel outside the front door, approaching the house.

'Quickly!' he muttered. 'Behind these curtains.'

Almost dragging the other bodily, he pushed him behind the thick black curtains that had been drawn tightly across the wide windows. There was the sound of muttered conversation in the hallway outside the room, coming nearer.

Cautiously, Nayland drew back the curtains a little way until he could see through the narrow slit between them. Two men entered the room and stood for a moment, looking about them.

Creoles! More of Caltro's men, no doubt.

He watched as they went over to the

altar, genuflected, then took down the sacred book and jeweled knife. They worked quietly and efficiently, clearly obeying instructions.

A moment later, after taking the book and knife out of the house, they were back, and took the richly embroidered cloth down from the altar itself, folding it carefully before going out of the room.

Nayland waited for a long moment, holding his breath. A second later, there was the sound of a powerful car starting up outside.

'Come on!' he snapped. 'Hurry! This may be the break we've been waiting for. I'm guessing they've been sent by Caltro to take these things to the place where they've got Simon a prisoner. With any luck, we ought to be able to follow them.'

Together, they made their way outside in time to see a small, but powerful-looking, car just vanishing along the almost deserted street. Nayland slipped in behind the wheel of his car, switched on the ignition.

Within seconds, Blake was beside him,

crushing into the seat and they were driving through the tall, wrought iron gates and along the street after the disappearing car.

Nayland concentrated on the steering of the speeding car as they turned a corner and spotted the other vehicle some three hundred yards ahead, gripping the wheel between his fingers until his hands began to ache with the strain. His stare was fixed on the road ahead, noting every twist and turn in the narrow street.

Inwardly, he thought: These people might be forced to wait until the time was favorable again, which meant they would still have a month or so in which to prepare a plan to rescue Simon. But in spite of this, he had the feeling that every minute they left Simon in the hands of these abominable creatures, they were increasing the danger to him

The car purred easily and more quickly now as they left the outskirts of the city behind and came out into the country. There were few other cars on the road and it was a relatively easy task to keep their quarry in view.

Nayland grew aware that the palms of his hands were cold and wet on the wheel of the car. Sweat lay in little patches on his back.

Blake said finally: 'I think they've seen us, Stephen.'

Nayland peered ahead. In the pouring rain, it was difficult to see properly but it did look as though the other car had suddenly put on a burst of speed and was drawing away from them. He pushed his foot down hard on the accelerator. Slowly, the intervening distance diminished.

'That's unfortunate,' he muttered harshly. 'If they have spotted us, they may have realized just who we are and they'll take us all over the country before they'll go anywhere near their hiding place.'

'He's trying his damnedest to shake us off,' Blake spoke thickly, pointing.

'Then maybe they're in a hurry to get to their destination,' gritted the other. 'If we can only stick with them, we may be able to force their hand.'

The car ahead was now less than a hundred yards away. One of the men in the speeding car suddenly turned, looking behind him. He moved his right hand in a queer little gesture and in that same instant, there was a brilliant flash of lightning followed almost instantly by an ear-splitting peal of thunder which seemed to rip open the very tissue of the air itself.

The flash half-blinded Nayland and instinctively, he jammed on the brakes, his hands jerking on the wheel and it was this involuntary action that undoubtedly saved their lives. A moment later, less than thirty yards ahead of them, a tall tree dropped directly in their path, blocking the road completely.

Nayland spun the wheel again, frantically, braking the car to a skidding halt less than three yards from the fallen tree. Beyond it, the car carrying Caltro's men and their sacred relics gathered speed and vanished into the storm. There came another mocking peal of thunder from almost directly overhead.

Getting out of the car, Nayland looked about him. The road here was so narrow that there was no way of making their way around the obstacle.

'Damn our rotten luck,' grumbled Blake as he surveyed the damage. 'Except for this accident, we might have caught up with them.'

'This was no accident,' Nayland said grimly.

'But the tree. It must have been hit by lightning. Surely you don't mean to say that they did it?'

'It's highly likely. I've seen men like Caltro able to direct storms and control the weather before.'

'But that's ridiculous. This was nothing more than sheer chance. Bad luck on our part.'

'Some time,' said Nayland, as they walked back to the car, 'you'll learn that what we call luck plays very little part in our lives. These things very rarely happen by chance. There always has to be a cause.'

Blake shrugged. 'Well, there's nothing for it now but to go back, I suppose.'

Backing the car to the very edge of the road, Nayland succeeded in turning it and they drove back slowly along the way

141

they had come. For the moment, it seemed, they had nothing to go on. Their only hope was that Caltro wouldn't try anything until the next full moon, but even that thought didn't help much now. There were far too many places in which he could have holed up. It would be like looking for a needle in a haystack.

At last they arrived back and after parking the car, they went inside.

'Did you discover where they've taken Mr. Merrivale, sir?' asked Sims.

Nayland shook his head. 'I'm afraid not, Sims. I don't think they'll harm him for a little while and at the moment, all that we have is the mask that came from Merrivale's house. Somehow, I think that lies at the bottom of this mystery.'

The manservant looked suddenly unhappy. 'I'm afraid that the mask is no longer here, sir. Mr. Caltro must have taken it with him this morning at the same time as Mr. Merrivale disappeared.'

'What?'

'That's right, sir. I knew you would want it when you got back so I made a point of looking for it. I can't find it anywhere.'

'Then if Caltro's got the mask and knows about the Voodoo on it, we're as good as finished,' Nayland said grimly.

8

The Transposition

The furniture had been removed from the large room and on the bare floor a chalk circle had been drawn large enough for two or three men to stand comfortably inside it. The tiny crystal cups containing holy water had been placed around the edge of the circle and there was a small incense burner sending out a cloud of pungent smoke that struck at Nayland's nostrils as he stood looking down at his handiwork.

Tall candles flickered at either side of the room and there were two inside the circle itself, giving off the only light in the room. Outside, the wildness of the storm gave an added eeriness to the scene.

Inside the circle itself, a hexagonal design had been drawn on the floor, also in chalk.

'Just what is it that you hope to do,

Stephen?' asked Blake doubtfully.

'We're going to use a little of Caltro's magic against him,' explained the other, 'to help us to locate Simon. This is something I dislike doing, but it's the only chance we've got. For ten days now, we've tried to find him, but without success. He's got to be somewhere and it's a fair chance that wherever he is, that accursed mask is also. It's going to help us to find this place where they're keeping him.'

'But surely that isn't possible?'

'Yes, it's possible, but dangerous.' He halted, angry at himself for the fear he felt clawing at his throat. 'You must follow all of my instructions carefully. Above all, once we have begun, you are not to step outside of the circle, nor let any part of you go outside, not even the tip of your finger. If you do, you're worse than a dead man, you'll be utterly lost. Do you understand that?'

Blake nodded. 'I think so. But I hope that you know what you're doing.'

'It's quite simple. I intend to transport your spirit, your mind if you like, to where the mask is. You'll find yourself looking through it, seeing the place where it is. Then, while the spell lasts, it will be up to you to describe the place, any distinguishing features so that we can locate it.'

'This doesn't seem right,' Blake said, looking doubtfully at Nayland. 'It's too — unscientific, to my mind. Maybe we ought to have called in the police. I'm sure they could have helped us.'

'Perhaps but not in time. If I know Caltro, he would kill Simon rather than allow him to return to us. He knows far too much already. No, this is the only way. Help me to set all of these things up. Then we'll be ready to begin.'

Carefully, he explained the procedure to the other, making sure that he understood it perfectly. With great precision, he marked out the pentagon on the floor and placed more cups of holy water at the points of the figure so that they entirely surrounded him, and placed a semi-circle of small golden candles around the central hexagon.

Finally, everything was ready, and

Nayland gave his final instruction to the other.

'While you're in the centre of the circle and before the transformation takes place, you may see shapes outside the ring. Ignore them if possible, but whatever you do, don't let them entice you out of the protective circle.

'This is black magic of a similar kind to that which Caltro uses to project his will onto others at a distance. The evil ones will gather, hoping to destroy us. They'll do everything to make us step out of the circle. Some may even take on the shape of people we know, perhaps even Simon, entreating us, imploring us to go to them, that everything is all right. Take no notice of them. It will only be a trick to get us outside to destroy us.'

He walked to the middle of the floor, inside the white chalk circle and Blake followed him.

'Good. Now you may sit down if you wish so long as no part of your body extends beyond the circle. And stay here whatever happens.'

Taking a deep breath, Nayland squared

his shoulders and began to recite the long, monotonous Latin phrases of the Zegrembi Incantation.

The shadows in the corners of the room, thrown huge and grotesque on the walls by the guttering candles, seemed to come alive, reaching down at them from all sides. He sensed, rather than felt, Blake move slightly into the very center of the circle.

There was a sudden roar of thunder almost directly overhead and the whole house shook to its very foundations.

Then the door of the room opened suddenly, unexpectedly, and Simon Merrivale stood there with a wild look on his face. There was blood oozing down his face from a gash on his cheek.

'Stephen! Richard!' His voice reached them above the rumble of the thunder. 'I made it. Quickly, they're close on my heels.'

Blake half-rose to his feet, but Nayland reached out and pulled him back.

'Don't be a fool,' he hissed. 'Can't you see that it isn't Simon, but some devil made up to look like him.'

'But it *is* Simon,' persisted Blake angrily. He almost tore himself from the other's restraining grasp, but Nayland held on wildly.

Gradually, the other sank back on to his knees inside the circle. There was a sudden shrill scream of rage and the thing in the doorway that had looked like Simon Merrivale suddenly faded away in a swirling of dark smoke and shadow.

The shadows in the room thickened. They now seemed to be pressing down against the tiny ring of lights that burned defiantly in the darkness. One of the candles flickered and threatened to go out although there was not the slightest breath of air in the room.

Then, gradually, about the chalk-marked circle there appeared to cluster in the smoke given off by the burning incense, a rank of dim, indistinct forms, shapes that were not quite human, yet resembling little else.

Nayland reached the end of the chant and turned to look at Blake. The other had suddenly become rigid; his features set and fixed. There was a look in his eyes that was like that of an idiot, vacant and empty, as though the soul had been removed from behind the eyes and only the empty shell of the body remained.

'Richard,' Nayland spoke loudly.

'Yes.' The word was a solitary whisper, scarcely heard.

'Can you feel anything?'

'There seems to be something over my face so that it's difficult to breathe.'

'The mask of Shabaka?'

'I think so.'

His voice sounded strangely muffled as if something dark, but invisible, were pushing down hard against his face. A sudden blast of icy air caught at the candle flames and one of them was snuffed out as though invisible fingers had plucked at it.

Leaping suddenly to his feet with a muttered curse of fear, Nayland lit it again with a long white taper from one of the other candles as the dark, hideous shapes, formed out of a coagulated nightmare, surged forward to cross the circle, straining against the protective barrier. There was a fearful, dreadful hunger in their movements that sent a shiver through Nayland's body.

'Can you see anything, Richard?' He spoke loudly and insistently to the other.

Blake's face twisted. 'I think I'm in a room, but it's difficult to see properly. There's a window in front of me looking out on the grounds of this place.'

'Go over to it.'

A brief pause, then the other said in a harsh voice, 'I can see out, but not very clearly.'

'Can you describe the grounds? Any feature which will tell us where this place might possibly be?'

Blake's lips moved slowly like those of a medium in a deep trance. 'I can see a long, double row of tall poplars at the far end of the grounds. There seems to be a road going past the end of the drive and a small village in the distance.'

The dark nightmare shapes around the chalk circle began to grow stronger with each succeeding second.

'Can you see anything else? Move around, leave the house if you can.'

The lips moved slowly in the waxen

face. 'It's raining hard out here on the lawn.'

A pause, then: 'I can see a sign at the end of the road, a little distance away.'

Nayland leaned forward. 'Keep going,' he hissed urgently. 'Try to read what it says.'

The eerie shapes solidified still further, began to fake on a definite form. Red glaring eyes stared balefully at him out of the shadows.

Blake appeared to be straining forward against something he couldn't see. Nayland fancied he could make out the dark, hazy outline of the mask and the feathered headdress around his companion's face, then the illusion was gone and Blake's features seemed normal again. His fingers were flexing and twitching uncontrollably by his sides, clenching and unclenching spasmodically. But Nayland knew that it wasn't really Blake who knelt there facing him; only the empty shell of the other's body. His spirit was somewhere far away, torn from his body by a magic as old as time itself, moving along a rain-soaked country lane in the wind and storm, searching for a clue which might lead them to Simon. One false move and it would be all over. Blake's mind and soul, divorced from his body, would never return, would be lost for ever somewhere out there in a grey limbo that had no meaning.

While his empty body, the face fixed in an imbecilic grin, would spend the rest of its days in some madhouse, completely and incurably insane.

A sense of urgency seized him.

'Hurry,' he whispered hoarsely. 'While the power lasts. There isn't much time.'

He grew aware that Blake was speaking again. 'I can just make out the words, but they're very indistinct. One of the words on the post is — Rodminster.'

'Rodminster — you're sure of that?'

'Yes.'

Nayland released his breath in a long, drawn-out sigh of relief. With an effort he pulled himself upright. There was a ring of triumph to his voice as he recited the monotonous Latin phrases.

Gradually, the flickering light from the ring of candles grew stronger. The dark, leaping shapes that strained from out of the corners, began to dim, to fade away. Outside, the storm, past its height, was moving slowly away towards the horizon.

He found that he was shivering slightly by the time he had finished the Incantation. Beside him, Blake stirred, looked about him scarcely comprehending, and then straightened up. He rubbed his face with a reflex gesture as though something had been irritating his skin.

'Didn't it succeed?' he asked slowly

Stiffly, Nayland got to his feet. 'It was touch and go,' he remarked calmly. 'Apparently, they've got Simon hidden away at some place called Rodminster. We'd better check on this place right away.'

In the library, Nayland took down the road map of the surrounding district and flipped through the pages rapidly.

'Ah, here we are. Rodminster. About thirty miles away. It looks as though we're on the right track after all.'

'What do you intend to do? Go down there right away?'

Nayland ran his fingers through his

hair. 'There's no sense in rushing in as we did the last time. We'll have to plan this thing carefully if we want to stay alive. We have one advantage over them so far. They don't know that we've managed to locate their hideout. Our best plan will be to go down there and put up in the village. There's bound to be an inn there no matter how small it is. We'd better make some discreet inquiries before we decide on any definite plan of action.'

'Right. When do we start?'

'We'll go down tomorrow. It should only take us an hour or so to get there. We'll leave in the afternoon and get there shortly before dark.

'We don't want too many inquisitive eyes watching us, but unless I miss guess, these people will be keeping themselves to themselves. They won't want to advertise their presence too much in case they attract undesirable attention.

'News will travel fast in a small village like this and there's bound to be gossip if anything out of the ordinary happens. These village folk never miss much of what goes on in their midst. One thing is worrying me, though. Chalka was meant to meet us at nine but that was almost an hour ago.'

Blake shrugged. 'Perhaps he decided to go after these people himself.'

'I sincerely hope not. If he has, he's a damned fool. Unfortunately, there's no time to go out and look for him. We can only hope he knows how dangerous these people are.'

★ ★ ★

Four o'clock in the afternoon. Darkness was already beginning to creep in from the eastern horizon. In the west, there was only a dull red glow, fading perceptibly, to indicate where the sun had been. Soon, it would be completely dark and the mist was even now beginning to swirl around the empty hedgerows on either side of the narrow, winding road. Silence wrapped itself tightly around the speeding car.

'You'd better check the map again, Richard,' said Nayland tersely. 'I'm sure we ought to have reached Rodminster by now, unless we've taken a wrong turning somewhere.'

A dark shadow jumped out into the light from the car headlights, swerved abruptly, and then skittered into the ditch on the opposite side of the road. Nayland pulled hard on the wheel cursing softly under his breath.

Blake leaned forward, bending over the road map spread out on his knee.

'If only we could come across some town or village, we might be able to get our bearings,' he said irritably. They seemed to have been travelling for hours without seeing a single light or house.

'We've got to reach some place pretty soon.' Blake lifted the map to see more clearly. 'We can't go on driving for ever without getting somewhere.'

Nayland nodded. It was stupid to begin getting alarmed simply because they had temporarily lost their way in the mist.

Ten minutes later, just as he was beginning to despair of ever seeing any sign of life again, they topped a low rise and saw a small village sprawled out below them.

'It looks as though we've arrived

somewhere at last,' he said, gripping the wheel tightly.

Blake glanced up from the map. 'Why this is the place I saw — ' He paused and rubbed a hand across his forehead. 'That's funny. I could have sworn I've seen this place before but I can't for the life of me remember where — or when.'

'Maybe you have seen it before,' said Nayland slowly. 'But not in the flesh.'

'You mean this is — Rodminster?'

'I think so.' He eased his foot on the accelerator and leaned back in his seat.

He slowed the car to a crawl and stopped it in front of the Inn. It was the only large three-storied building in the entire village. There were lights in the windows and the quiet murmur of soft music. He opened the door and got out.

'This looks like a fairly decent place to stay,' muttered Blake.

Nayland grinned and stretched his cramped limbs. 'It looks the only place,' he corrected. 'I telephoned the landlord yesterday so he'll be expecting us.'

The door creaked a little as he pushed

it open and went inside and for some unaccountable reason the sound sent a little tremor through him. But inside, there was a warm log fire burning in the wide hearth and bright lights which hurt their eyes a little after the darkness outside

The innkeeper, a tall, bronzed man with a cheerful open face came to meet them and took their cases from them.

'Good evening, gentlemen,' he said heartily. 'Mr Nayland and Mr Blake, I presume?'

Nayland nodded. 'That's right,' he said slowly. He went over to the roaring fire and held his chilled hands out to the flames. Slowly, some of the warmth was beginning to come back into his body

'I'll see that your bags are taken up to your rooms,' the landlord said. 'Meanwhile I suppose you'll be wanting something hot to eat.

'It isn't often that we have visitors here at this time of the year. A very quiet place but in the summer things are different. Now, you'll have the place all to yourselves, except in the evenings, of course, when some of the regulars drop in, you know.'

Nayland stood looking about him. Everything seemed so sane and normal here, with the fire crackling in the hearth and the bright lights shining off the glass bottles at the back of the bar. It was difficult to believe that, if their guesses were anywhere near the truth, terrible things were being planned only a short distance away.

The landlord went out with their bags and returned a few moments later with a couple of glasses. 'Something to warm you up after your journey, gentlemen,' he said jovially. 'I'll have a meal ready for you in a few minutes. I trust you had a good trip down.'

'We thought we were lost at one time,' Nayland said. 'I suppose we must have taken a wrong turning some distance back.'

'That's easily done, sir, especially at this time of the year. It seems to get dark so suddenly and it's quite simple to make a mistake.' He looked curiously at them for a long moment, then went on: 'Tell me, gentlemen, if it isn't too impertinent a question: Why did you come down here to Rodminster? Surely it wasn't for pleasure — not in December.'

Nayland glanced up sharply but there was no expression on the other's face. Yet there had been something in his voice that made him pause. Almost as if the other knew why they were there, or had guessed it, and wanted to confirm his suspicions.

'In a way we're combining business with pleasure,' he said evasively, choosing his words carefully. 'As a matter of fact, this village was recommended to us as a quiet place where we could get away from everything for a little while.'

It sounded a lame reply and he had the idea that there was a sharp look of disbelief on the other's face.

'I see, sir. Of course.' The landlord sounded uneasy. 'I merely thought that you might be here because — ' he broke off suddenly.

'Because what?' prompted Blake.

The landlord hesitated for a long moment, then: 'I thought you might be down here from London in connection with those strange goings-on at the old Lowrey place.'

'The Lowrey place?' asked Nayland. 'Why — what's been happening there?'

The other seemed suddenly ill at ease. 'It's nothing really, I suppose. If that isn't the reason why you came here, maybe I oughtn't to talk about it.'

'Maybe you *had* better tell us about it,' suggested Nayland. 'It may have some bearing on why we're here.'

It was now the landlord's turn to look surprised. When he spoke again, his voice was guarded and he changed the subject completely. 'I'll go and see whether your meal is ready yet, gentlemen.'

He left the room, closing the door softly behind him.

'I knew it!' said Blake hoarsely. 'They have got Simon here and they're holding him prisoner at this Lowrey place somewhere outside the village.'

'Don't jump to conclusions,' warned Nayland. 'We don't know anything for certain. We'd better get the landlord to talk before we decide anything. Maybe a few of the other villagers could tell us something of what's been happening too.'

'But at least we know that there's something wrong.'

Somewhere in the distance, a door opened quietly and there was the low murmur of hushed conversation. A moment later the door closed again and when the landlord returned, his face was grey and strained with a look of horror that he couldn't hide.

'Something wrong?' asked Nayland, a sudden sinking feeling in the pit of his stomach

The other nodded sickly. 'That was Bert Cowdrey, one of the gamekeepers around here. They've just discovered the body of a man up on the edge of the moors less than a quarter of a mile from here. They say he was in a horrible mess when they found him.'

'Any idea who he was?' asked Blake harshly.

The landlord shook his head. 'He wasn't a local man and they haven't identified him so far, sir. In fact, I don't know whether they ever will. You see, he wasn't a white man at all, he was a Negro!'

Nayland felt the surging horror leap inside him. The nightmare came back with a vengeance.

9

The Thing That Kills

Brushing aside the landlord's protests about the spoiled meal, Nayland and Blake left the inn and made their way along the narrow, winding street which led upward towards the low hill to the south of the village. Gradually, they left the houses behind and came out into the country, following the instructions that the landlord had given to them.

Nayland didn't want to believe what he felt inside. It was just possible that he was wrong about the identity of the man who had been killed, but he didn't think so.

'You're thinking that maybe this murdered man is Chalka, the man who came to see us about the mask and headdress,' said Blake after an uneasy pause.

'Maybe it won't be, but I've an awful suspicion that it is. If so, why did they kill him?'

Blake rubbed his chin in thoughtful silence, then said soberly, 'My guess would be that after he left in the morning, Chalka remained close to the house, possibly waiting for us to leave, thinking he might get his hands on the mask and headdress but instead Caltro turned up and took them.'

Nodding in agreement, Nayland added, 'So obviously Chalka somehow followed them to Rodminster.'

They walked on in silence. A little further on, they saw the narrow path that led off the road into the blackness of the trees. There were lights at the far edge of the moors and Nayland felt his feet lurch and bump over loose stones as they walked upon the path.

The smell of the undergrowth was sharp in their nostrils, catching at the back of their throats. Ahead of them there was a small group of men standing on the edge of the wood, just visible in the curling mist.

They glanced round as Nayland and Blake approached. Briefly, Nayland introduced Blake and himself, and explained that they had just arrived in the inn and had heard of the trouble from the landlord and come along to see if they could be of any assistance.

If the others resented them pushing their way in like this, none of them gave any outward sign. One man, who introduced himself as Dr. Reeves, said quickly, but with a touch of horror in his voice:

'I've never seen anything like this before in my whole career as a doctor. It's utterly horrible. His whole body has been ripped and torn as though by a knife or fangs, almost as if he had been attacked by some wild beast.'

'Then that was the cause of his death?' said Nayland.

He walked forward and peered down at the still body, looking into the dead face that stared up at him, unseeing. There was an expression blended of utter horror and fear stamped on the man's waxen features that was shocking to see. He went down on one knee beside him, being careful to touch nothing.

One glance was sufficient to tell him

that it was, indeed, Chalka. The lips were thinned over the teeth and the eyes held a horror beyond all imagining as though they had looked upon things that were not fit for human sight.

'Poor devil,' he said, straightening up. He looked his question at the doctor.

The other shook his head. 'This may sound incredible, I know,' he said helplessly, 'but it's my opinion that these wounds were not the cause of death. I know he looks as though he's been cut into pieces in parts, but I'd say offhand that he died of fright.'

'Fright, doctor?' One of the men in police uniform, looked up incredulously. 'But that's impossible, unless it's something to do with — '

He finished his sentence with a slight shudder that Nayland noticed immediately.

'You think there may be something more to it than just fright then?' Nayland asked, turning to the officer. The mad sensation of panic was leaving him now, fading away slowly.

The doctor cut in angrily. 'There has

been quite a lot of talk in the village during the past several days,' he said smoothly, obviously hiding something. 'All rumors, nothing more, I can assure you.'

'Then you really think this is the work of a maniac?'

'What else?' The other shrugged his shoulders with a gesture that said more than mere words. 'Can you give me any other *logical* explanation?'

Nayland noticed the way the doctor laid particular stress on the one word. He sensed that this wasn't the first inexplicable thing that had happened in this tiny village, but was rather the dreadful culmination of a lot of frightening things that, as the doctor seemed to believe, were better not discussed.

'I think there may be quite a lot of possible explanations, doctor,' he said carefully, 'although I doubt whether you, as a medical man, would believe any of them.'

'So Gregg has been talking again, has he?'

'Gregg?'

'The landlord. I thought I told him to keep his mouth shut about these things.'

'But whatever they are, you can't keep them quiet for ever.' There was a note of exasperation in Nayland's voice. 'This,' — he indicated the body lying at their feet — 'will have to come out into the open. You can't hush up murder no matter how you think it might have been committed.'

'I don't intend to hush up murder, Mr. Nayland,' remarked the police constable icily. 'All that I am trying to do is to stamp out these ridiculous rumors which have been circulating in the village ever since the Lowrey mansion was occupied a couple of weeks ago.'

'Black Magic?' prompted Nayland.

The other looked at him curiously, then nodded 'Yes — that's right,' he admitted. 'Why, what do you know about it?'

'A little,' said Nayland pointedly. 'But I think if possible Doctor Reeves and I ought to have a talk before this goes any further. I think it would prove interesting and enlightening to both of us.'

The doctor sighed. 'Very well, Mr. Nayland, come to my surgery tomorrow afternoon about four o'clock. I think you know a lot more about this affair than you're saying.'

Turning to Blake after the doctor had gone, Nayland said harshly, 'It looks to me as though they discovered Chalka, possibly while he was attempting to retrieve the mask and headdress and he was attacked.'

'By Shabaka you mean?'

'No.' Nayland shook his head emphatically. 'From the look of those injuries I would say it was far more likely that he was attacked by Caltro.'

'Caltro!'

'That's right. He has more powers than you could dream of. One of them is lycanthropy.'

'You mean he's a werewolf?'

'Exactly.'

★   ★   ★

Early the following afternoon, they visited Dr Reeves. Rodminster was not a very large community. Nayland had the impression of small buildings, crowded

171

very much together, huddled as if for warmth and protection around the small square in the middle of the village.

They turned into the small, well-kept garden fronting the doctor's house. Nayland knocked sharply on the glass-paneled door, then opened it as a voice called on them to enter. They went inside, Nayland closing the door gently behind him, meanwhile studying the man who had risen to his feet as they entered. A tall man, slightly-built, with iron-grey hair and brown eyes that studied them curiously in return.

'Well, gentlemen, come inside. Sit down and make yourselves comfortable.'

Nayland slid into the tall, comfortably-padded chair that stood across the desk from the doctor. Blake lowered himself into the other chair a couple of feet away.

'Doctor Reeves,' Nayland began hesitantly, 'I realize that a first interview like this is likely to be a little difficult for you. No doubt, you've probably guessed why we're here, in Rodminster, but I'd like to make the position quite clear to you from the very beginning. It isn't going to be very easy for you to believe what we're going to tell you.'

'You mean about Black Magic?'

'Exactly. You're a doctor, so I gather that you don't believe in such things.'

'No, Mr. Nayland. I strongly disbelieve in them. I don't think you'll be able to convince me of any truth in the supernatural. Not unless I see some of these things with my own eyes.'

'Then what about that dead man on the moors last night?' interrupted Blake.

'I examined the body quite thoroughly later,' the doctor remarked stiffly. 'All of the available evidence was sufficient to support my original argument. Something — or someone — attacked him, inflicting such severe lacerations to the head and body that even if they weren't enough to kill him outright, the shock would do so.'

'It may interest you to know that we knew this man,' said Nayland.

The other rubbed his chin thoughtfully. 'Somehow, I gained that impression last night,' he said. 'That's one of the reasons why I agreed so readily to this meeting.'

'His name was Chalka. He visited me

about a fortnight ago, concerning some relics which he claimed had been stolen from his tribe in the African jungle and brought over to London.'

'Just what were these relics, Mr. Nayland?'

'The mask and headdress of Shabaka, one of their earliest witchdoctors. He claimed there was a voodoo associated with them; a curse placed on them by Shabaka when he was treacherously slain. Anyone who came into contact with them when the moon was either full, or I believe now in a certain position in the heavens, became inhabited by the soul of the witchdoctor. *Indeed, it's my belief that while wearing these relics at these particular times they actually become this witchdoctor!*'

'And you believe this foolishness?' The doctor uttered a harsh laugh.

'I've seen too many of these inexplicable things happen not to believe in them. But that's beside the point. What is important from our point of view is that we know what has been happening here during the past two weeks.'

'Very well, I'll tell you all I know,' said the other. He leaned back in his chair. 'To the best of my knowledge, it all began about a fortnight ago. The old mansion near the top of the hill has been empty for many years. The last of the Lowrey family died almost thirty years ago and I doubt whether anybody has lived in it since. It's an evil place, with an equally evil reputation.

'That's why we were all surprised to learn that someone had taken it for the winter and intended living there. I don't actually remember who started the rumors although it was probably one of the gamekeepers on the estate. Something about a dark, hideous shape running loose in the woods if I remember correctly. At first, we put it down to his imagination. Moonlight and shadows can play tricks with you at night when you're all alone. We searched the woods of course, just in case there was anything out of the ordinary there, and found very little to pay us for our trouble.'

'Ah, but there was *something*?' interposed Nayland.

175

'Well, there were tracks in the under-growth especially where the rain had turned it into mud. They showed that someone had been there recently.'

'What kind of tracks were they?'

'Human footprints,' said the other. 'Someone had been running in the woods in their bare feet.'

Nayland shivered. Bare feet! Only a native would do that naturally, his mind told him. *A witchdoctor?* Was he correct in believing that Shabaka actually rein-carnated himself once he had taken over a host's body? It certainly looked that way.

'There have been other rumours too, of course. Some don't make much sense at all, and one in particular I've never been able to understand.'

'Maybe you'd better tell us about it,' suggested Nayland. 'There's just a chance that it could be important and may throw some light on the whole thing.'

'Very well, if you wish. It happened about seven nights ago. A young couple was returning from a dance in Melchester about twelve miles away. Their car broke down somewhere along the road, quite near to the Lowrey house. It was moonlight and so they decided that rather than wait for some other car to come along, a rather unlikely occurrence at that time in the morning, they would walk it back into Rodminster, a matter of a mile or so.

'I want you to understand that, so far, we've only been able to piece together what happened from what we've been able to learn from the man. His wife, when we found her, was in a state of profound shock, bordering on coma. At the present time, she's in the nearby hospital undergoing treatment.

'They were making their way along the road which leads past the old mansion, when they noticed a light flickering in one of the windows — '

'Like a candle-flame,' suggested Nayland.

'That's almost exactly how he described it to us when we questioned him later. They stopped to watch for a few minutes. At that time, neither of them knew that the house had been taken and thought at first that it was somebody sleeping there for the night — a tramp, probably.'

'Did either of them go inside to see?' asked Blake

'No, I gather they thought better of it, perhaps because it was none of their business anyway, and they were anxious to get home and report what had happened to their car.

'It was just as they reached the end of the road that they noticed something lying in the bushes. Here the man's story becomes hard to believe. He says they walked forward to have a closer look, thinking that it was an injured animal of some kind and found that it was a mask and a peculiar headdress made of skin and feathers.

'The man swears that the things moved of their own volition. There was no wind so that wasn't the explanation. They apparently scuttled over the ground towards them. He shouted a warning to his wife to run and tried to drag her along the road towards the village, away from the trees. Then he says, he looked back to see why she seemed to be resisting him and saw that — '

The doctor hesitated at that point and shrugged helplessly.

'Go on,' prompted Nayland tensely.

'He says that something indescribable happened to his wife, as soon as those things came into contact with her. She — well, she changed.'

'Ah, so there we have it.' Nayland stood up and took a quick, nervous turn about the room. 'It means that as far as Simon is concerned, we may have less time than we thought.'

Dr. Reeves looked up at him curiously. 'Just what are you talking about. Mr. Nayland?' he asked.

'These people who've taken the old house on the edge of the village are preparing for the ceremony of the Black Mass.'

'The Black Mass!' The doctor looked shocked. 'But surely such superstition can't still exist nowadays?'

'It can exist — and does. I myself have seen it at work more than once. It may surprise you, doctor, to know that in this country alone, there are thousands of people, outwardly men and women like ourselves, who celebrate these evil and obscene rites.'

'But how on Earth can you be so sure?'

'Quite easily. You see, these ceremonies are often celebrated by an unfrocked priest or someone who has risen among them to the rank of Grand Ipsissimus. They must use a silver chalice which has been consecrated in some church and then stolen — and these thefts can be ascertained through the usual channels.'

'But why do they do it?' muttered the doctor, sinking deeper into his chair. 'Surely they can't be completely sane, these people?'

Nayland shrugged. 'As to their sanity, doctor, I'm afraid that I'm not a competent person to judge their condition, but from what I know of them personally, they do it for a great many reasons. Many of them have lost their loved ones and almost all of them, at some time or another, had prayed earnestly to God to bring them back safely, or deliver them from illness.

'But their prayers went unanswered, and their loved ones died. That's why these people turned their faces away from God and all He stands for and became easy prey for such inhuman monsters as these. If God wouldn't listen to you and give you what you asked for, they are told, then the Devil would. He could give you anything you desired.'

'It's feasible, I suppose, when you put it that way,' agreed the doctor.

'Too feasible, I'm afraid,' muttered Nayland. 'But unlike Christianity, or any of the other religions, they can't back out of it whenever they wish. These people rule by fear and horror — and the trouble is that most of the tales you hear about the power possessed by their High Priests of Satan are true.

'The majority of their converts are ordinary men and women. But the true adherents to this evil faith, the men who have crossed the abyss and attained the position of Grand Ipsissimus, possess great powers of darkness and evil.'

'And you really believe all of this, Mr. Nayland?'

'I've seen it all for myself,' said the other simply. 'I know.'

'Then all I can say is that you're either a fool or a very brave man, Mr Nayland, and somehow, I can't bring myself to believe that you're a fool.'

'Do you think that you could help us, doctor?' Nayland asked deliberately.

'I'm not quite sure how I can. What you've said has been extremely interesting, I'll admit, but scarcely the kind of thing a country doctor could dabble with.'

'We'll put our cards on the table, doctor,' Nayland said. 'A friend of ours, Simon Merrivale, has been taken by force from his home in London and brought here by these people. From what little evidence we have and from what you've just told us, it's quite obvious they're holding him prisoner in this old mansion near the village.

'We've good reason to believe that a man named Ernest Caltro is preparing to conduct the Black Mass in order that he may become a Grand Ipsissimus. This, I ought to tell you, requires a human sacrifice and we believe that Simon Merrivale is destined to be the victim.

'Unless we can get him away from there very soon, I'm afraid that they'll kill him. They tried once before, but we heard of it and managed to prevent it. This time, they've been forewarned and it isn't going to be so easy.'

'But if they've taken him away by force, why don't you go to the police?'

'I'm afraid that wouldn't solve anything,' Nayland said tautly. 'If they didn't kill him out of hand before the police arrived to prevent it, they would have him safely locked away somewhere where no one could find him and you can't do anything to these people without evidence.

'So far, we only have circumstantial evidence that there's something strange happening here. Imagine what the police would say if we told them that this man, Caltro, was going to carry out the ceremony of the Black Mass at full moon with Merrivale as the sacrifice. They'd laugh at us or lock us away in a madhouse.'

'Then what do you propose to do?'

'Somehow we have got to get in there

without being seen and get Merrivale away. I think it's also important that we get hold of this mask and headdress. The sooner they're returned to their rightful place, the sooner we'll put an end to the evil associated with them.'

'And if these people discover you?'

'That's another thing you can do to help us. We'll need protection against them. I don't mean guns and things. Those aren't the weapons they normally use. If we can get some holy water and a piece of the Sacred Host from the local priest, it will afford us the greatest protection possible.'

The doctor was silent for a moment, then he said slowly: 'Mr Nayland, I don't know why I believe you, but somehow I do. If there is anything in what you've told me, then I agree that the sooner we stamp it out, the better.

'Your method may be unorthodox to say the least, but if it works, then it will have served its purpose. I'll see Father Handon this evening and put your request to him. If you could come and see me first thing tomorrow morning, I'll let you know what the position is.'

'Thank you, doctor.' Nayland moved towards the door with Blake. He felt a little easier in his mind, but there was still that little voice of fear, deep down, muttering inside his brain.

10

The Dark Ones

Stephen Nayland stood at the end of the long, overgrown drive where the path ran steep and straight up the hillside and looked again at the great, dark building, stark and oddly unreal, that stood perched on the side of the hill.

Up there, above the village, a mile from the small houses that nestled as if for warmth where the roads crossed, the Lowrey mansion looked grim and forbidding, turreted and towered like some medieval castle. It looked exactly as he imagined it would, just the sort of place Caltro would have chosen for his diabolical plans.

Beside him, Blake stirred uneasily and a couple of feet away, clearly uncomfortable, although he was doing his best not to show it, stood the doctor,

'I trust that you know what you're

doing, Mr. Nayland,' he said. 'It's only because I don't believe in these demons of yours, and that I don't want to see you making a fool of yourself when you try to break into this house, that I agreed to come.'

'Don't underestimate these fiendish creatures,' Nayland said, keeping his voice low. 'They may look human to you when you see them for the first time, but that's only a devilishly clever act of theirs to lull the unwary into a state of false security. But at least we've got the protection of the Sacred Host, thanks to you, doctor.'

'From what I was able to gather from the priest, he seems to think there may be something in what you say. Whether he really believes all this superstitious non-sense about black magic, I'm not sure. But he seemed quite willing to allow you to have some of the host and holy water.'

Directly in front of them, reaching up to the moonlit sky, were the tall poplars that Blake had described so accurately during that brief spell inside the circle and the pentagon.

There were no lights showing in the

house and to all intents and purposes it seemed empty, utterly deserted, the home of rats and spiders and nothing more. But, looking at it, Nayland felt a little shiver of fear pass through him. Unless he was gravely mistaken, the place was more crowded now than at any other time in its evil history.

Peopled by creatures in human shape but intent on inhuman practices, he wondered vaguely what was going on in there at that very moment. There was the feel of eyes watching them from the darkness — evil, unfriendly eyes, peering at them from the curtained windows, following their every move, plotting their destruction.

'All right,' said Nayland. 'We'll gain nothing by standing here in the moonlight. Let's go. But be careful!'

Deliberately, he thrust his way forward. The wind was suddenly a savage force, tearing at his coat, threatening to hurl him back along the path, clutching at him with savage, ripping fingers, shrieking past his ears, stinging his face. For a brief instant, the sharp smell of the pine needles in the undergrowth beneath their feet gave way to something foul and decaying and rotten that clutched at the back of his throat, almost choking him.

For an instant, he was taken by surprise. Madly, he fought off the illusion, recognizing it for what it was. There was a moment when he was almost suffocated, then the smell was gone, leaving him gasping for breath, a little unsure as to whether or not he had simply imagined it all.

The moon suddenly broke free of the swarming clouds which had appeared as though from nowhere to engulf it; and there was a flooding of pale light all around them again.

It took all of his willpower to keep from glancing continually over his shoulder, expecting to see a multitude of black shapes coming after him, hunting them down in the moonlight — creatures conjured up by Caltro.

He moistened his lips and turned his head a little towards the others, stumbling along behind him. 'They know that we're coming,' he said thinly. 'That was only a

189

foretaste of what they'll do to stop us from getting Simon back.'

'Do you think they'll kill him out of hand now that they know we're here?' Blake asked.

'I don't think so,' Nayland muttered. 'It's likely that Caltro will decide to go through with the Black Mass tonight, hoping to hold us off until it's completed.'

He almost stumbled over the body before he saw it. He tensed as he recognized the upturned face that stared up at him, etched by the moonlight with a multitude of tiny shadows.

Blake peered over his shoulder. 'God — it's Simon!'

'Your friend?' The doctor came forward hurriedly and looked down. 'But he's badly hurt. We'll have to get him back to the village and attend to him at once.'

'He must have got away from them somehow,' said Blake. He went down on one knee and rolled the other over. 'He still seems to be alive. Now, thank God, there's no need to go through with this affair. We can — '

'No!' Nayland spoke so suddenly and

so savagely that the other two stared round at him in surprise.

'This isn't Simon. It's just another diabolical trick to throw us off the scent. They're afraid of us this time if they have to resort to things like this.'

'But it *is* Simon!' persisted Blake. 'Why good God man, you've only got to look at him to see.'

'I tell you it's not him!' Nayland's fingers closed over the tiny silver container in which had been placed the Sacred Host. Be calm and methodical, he told himself fiercely as he strove to control and discipline his will.

He looked down at the body sprawled at their feet. Even in the moonlight, it seemed to glow a little with a rippling greenish phosphorescence. Then, as he watched, it began to fade away, slowly at first, then rapidly, until there was nothing there.

'Good Lord,' the doctor whispered. 'I could have sworn that — '

Nayland smiled mirthlessly. 'Now, perhaps, you're beginning to see what we're up against, doctor. And I think you'll see more terrifying and inexplicable things than that before this night is through.'

It was very quiet in the chill moonlight as they made their way slowly towards the house. Ahead of them, the path wound across the overgrown lawn until it ended at the house itself, now less than thirty yards away.

Quite suddenly, from somewhere in the blackness of the shrouding shadows in front of them, quite close at hand, there came the unmistakable trill of thin, malicious laughter. It was a strangely evil, threatening sound. Slowly it faded away.

Then, abruptly, Nayland was aware of someone standing in front of them, less than six feet away. One minute the lawn had been deserted, the next, this small man dressed in the black robes of a priest stood facing them, one arm upraised a little.

Doctor Reeves started forward. 'Why, Father Handon, I understood that you wouldn't be able to come.'

'I came to warn you not to go into that house,' said the little priest slowly, his words clear and distinct. Nayland was suddenly aware just how quiet it had all become and the realization put him on his guard instantly.

'There is terrible evil there which can destroy you, even with the protection you have. I must urge you to go back and wait. It is dangerous for you to attempt anything tonight.'

'Very well, Father,' said the doctor hoarsely. He turned to face Nayland. 'I told you it was foolish to go on with this. I suggest we take Father Handon's word for it and return to the village.'

'This isn't Father Handon any more than I am!' snapped Nayland. 'They're doing their damnedest to get us to leave. That means they're afraid of something. And the only thing that a man like Caltro will be afraid of, is something breaking into the middle of the Black Mass with something as powerful as what I have in my pocket.'

'But I — '

The doctor stopped suddenly. There was a shrill screech of thwarted anger and the thing that had looked like Father

Handon flowed away into something else and then vanished completely.

As quickly as he could, Nayland walked forward over the wet grass of the lawn. He glanced down at his watch. Ten minutes to midnight. So little time, muttered a little voice in his brain, already they would have begun their obscene ceremony.

He stopped. There was that nameless odor of filth and decay around him again sending his heart jumping, hammering into his throat. He could sense that the others were feeling the same way.

'Keep close to me,' he warned in a harsh whisper. 'And above all, if you see anything, don't panic. That could be fatal. We have sufficient protection for anything we may come up against so long as we keep our wits about us. There won't be a second chance if we fail tonight.'

They reached the door, strong and massive, barred with strips of metal.

'Look!' The doctor pointed a finger upwards.

A light was flickering in one of the windows. An eerie glow that seemed to pulse and waver, never remaining steady for any length of time.

'Quickly,' Nayland muttered. 'There's no time to be lost.' He made to pull the gun from his pocket. There seemed to be some strong, invisible force holding him back, thrusting his arm down to his side as he lifted the gun, placed it close to the lock of the heavy door and pulled the trigger. There was a deafening report that woke all of the echoes around the house. The lock shattered and the door swung open as he thrust against it madly with his shoulder.

Together, they tumbled inside, into darkness. Not a single light was visible.

'Hurry! We've got to find them while there's still time.'

Something rustled darkly in one of the corners, peering at them out of red eyes filled with a naked hatred There was a flicker of motion and then the thing was gone.

They became aware of a quiet, low voice murmuring monotonously in the emptiness of the house. Nayland twisted his head round sharply to determine from which direction the voice came, but found it impossible.

'It came from over there. I'm sure of it,' Reeves said, switching on the torch he'd brought, and swinging the beam across the room to dimly reveal the foot of a staircase through an open doorway.

One after the other, they hurried across the room their feet clattering on the wooden floorboards.

The monotonous voice was louder now, more insistent and Nayland could hear others joining in with it at intervals. But still he was unable to make out the words. It was all he could do to force his legs to move. They seemed to have become turned to water, unable to bear his weight. But he had to move, to get Simon away from this place if there was still a chance.

They reached the foot of a wide stairway which led up to the rooms above, sweeping around a gentle curve halfway up; there was a pale slit of yellow light, just visible, at the top.

Nayland pulled himself forward, staggering up the stairs sensing rather than seeing the others following closely behind him. Vaguely, he was aware of the doctor's harsh breathing and the sound of his own heart beating in his ears.

'This way,' he shouted, raising his voice to make himself heard above the shrieking chant which burst forth from somewhere above them. The murmur of voices seemed to have lost its pleading tone. Now there was a triumphant ring to it that frightened him.

With an effort, he reached the top of the stairs and looked about him to get his bearings.

The voices had dropped into silence for a moment and he could hear nothing. Then, they began again, a throbbing insistent mutter of sound that rose in crescendo. The doctor swung his torch beam. It revealed a door on one side of a long passage.

'In there!' Nayland rapped, lunging forward, and twisting the handle of the door. It was locked.

The sound of the shot as he blew the lock to pieces, was scarcely audible above the chanting voices. He felt a little thrill of horror pass through him as he put his weight against the door and heaved it open, almost falling into the room beyond, carried forward by his own momentum.

In appearance, the room was similar to that which he had seen back at Simon Merrivale's house. It was, if anything, larger, the ceiling a curved immensity high overhead, painted a brilliant scarlet so that it seemed to his stultified vision that he was looking directly into the Pit of Hell.

Then his vision righted itself and he saw that it was only the result of a very clever artistic design, cunningly contrived, which gave the appearance of depth when viewed obliquely.

A vast erection of carved stone stood at the far end of the room, hung with heavy, richly-embroidered curtains of black and gold, topped with glittering crystal and silver vases and cups. Ernest Caltro, easily recognizable even from that distance, stood with his back to them, his arms raised slightly as if in prayer.

But this, Nayland knew instinctively,

was no prayer to a Christian God. Out of the corner of his eye, he caught a fragmentary glimpse of the doctor and Blake staring into the room, their eyes wide.

There must have been at least a score of other people in the room. All were kneeling on the hard floor, facing the altar. Many of them, Nayland noticed, were women. They all wore white gowns, trimmed with black velvet and their faces, what little he could see of them in the light, were set into lines of utter concentration, their eyes filled with a feral eagerness.

'The Black Mass,' Nayland said unnecessarily.

Ernest Caltro was a tall, bloated figure, standing perfectly still, his arms upraised, his head thrown back a little way, intoning the monotonous phrases which seemed to move on to the air in little flashes of lambent flame.

At first, Nayland could see no sign of Simon. Then, as his eyes became accustomed to the light, he made out the inert figure of the other, lying on the stone altar, almost completely hidden by the corpulent bulk of Caltro's body. The jeweled knife lay a little way from his feet and the silver chalice had been placed at his head.

One of the women came forward and stepped up behind Caltro. There was something soft and flowing in her hands and she draped it carefully over the other's shoulders. The lights dimmed slightly and then resumed their original strength. The weird chant began again and occasionally Caltro would lower his hands and make some strange sign in the air in front of his face, at times making obeisance to the altar.

'What in God's name are they going to do?' Reeve's voice shook a little and his face looked ghastly in the greenish glow. 'And why haven't they seen us before this?'

'Maybe they didn't hear us, maybe they're in some kind of trance — ' Nayland broke off. At the far end of the room, Caltro had ascended the altar, his arms wide. Then, he turned and faced his audience.

His green features, lit by the ghostly radiance were satanic and oddly diabolical. Like the Devil Incarnate, thought Nayland, his fingers closing around the silver container with the Sacred Host. Madly, he strove to control his reeling senses. There was a sudden roar in his ears, almost blotting out everything else.

Caltro moved forward slowly until he stood at the bottom of the altar. Behind him, there was a sudden wavering as of black smoke; a mist, a fog, something that initially had no shape, but which thickened and whirled, forming, forming . . .

11

The Devil Incarnate

It took all of Nayland's control to prevent himself from crying out at what he saw next. Vaguely, he was aware of Blake's sharp intake of breath and the low moan that escaped the doctor's lips. The thing at the end of the room, above the huge altar became something more than mist. There was substance and something evil like a dark shadow standing out hellishly against the greenness.

He was aware that Caltro was shouting words at the top of his voice and that this time, he was able to understand them quite clearly. They seemed to enter his brain as though each were coated with acid.

'Once again, the Grand Master has come. We must begin our sacrifice. We must all renew the vows of obedience we made.' He made a sharp movement with the forefinger of his right hand.

Above the altar, a rearing goat shape looked down at the gathering out of slitted eyes. A terrible triumphant neighing filled the entire room, seeming to shake the house to its very foundations like a peal of thunder.

Then, Caltro looked up and in that single instant, they were seen. The Goat clashed its hooves together and sparks flew from its eyes. Its foetid breath reached Nayland even across the width of the room.

'The sacrifice must go on,' screamed Caltro at the top of his voice. 'But now we have more victims to give in sacrifice to our Master.'

Nayland fumbled blindly in his pocket. His fingers were slippery with sweat and the silver container kept sliding out of his grasp just when he thought he had a tight hold on it. The green glare hampered his vision, but he had a vague impression of the people in the gathering turning to face them, come running forward, their eyes afire with an eager hatred.

Meanwhile, beyond them, in front of

the altar, Caltro had seized the sacrificial knife and was holding it poised above Simon's body as he lay on his back on the altar.

'No! God — no!' Desperately, Nayland tried to shout the words, but they refused to come.

Caltro's voice was droning somewhere in the background. 'Now receive thy victim O Prince of Darkness. Claim that body and soul which is rightfully yours. For your existence shall be his existence; your being, his being. And the bond which shall be forged between you by this sacred knife shall remain unbroken until the end of time.'

The vast, rearing beast suddenly drew itself up on to its hind legs, towering above the altar. The slitted eyes flashed fire, the cloven hooves crashed with a sound like thunder. The terrible neighing bleat echoed in Nayland's ears, drowning out the sound of his own voice as he tried to pray.

Desperately, he fumbled in his pocket, then succeeded in drawing out the tiny silver casket. Out of the corner of his eye, he was aware of one of the women, walking forward towards Caltro; and for the first time, he noticed the mask and headdress which he had been seeking for so long, lying on the altar beside the red book which lay open on a silver stand.

Now it was clear that Caltro could take these objects whenever he wished without Merrivale's permission. Obviously here, the power of the Goat of Mendes was far greater than any spell that had been placed upon them.

Taking up the mask and headdress, Caltro handed them to the woman as she turned and faced the altar. Her features changed, blurred a little, then became those of Shabaka, the witch-doctor.

With a swiftly uncalculated action like a reflex kick, Nayland succeeded in lifting the tiny casket in front of him, his fingers fumbling with the catch. The Sacred Host was their only hope now. He must open the catch. There was not a single moment to lose. Already, the vast figure of the Goat of Mendes was reaching up over the altar. The knife held in Caltro's hand was beginning to flash downwards towards Simon's unprotected body.

Something foul and rotten touched his face. A hand seemed to reach out of the greenness and clutch at his fingers, pulling them away, tearing them apart, so that he almost dropped the silver container.

Then the catch clicked open. Instantly a ray of pure white light seemed to stream up into the room. The greenness faded, writhed away from the brilliance.

Weakly, he held it up so that it was in full view of the men and women in front of him. They turned and began to scream thinly in terror, running this way and that in all directions, striving to get out of the way of that pure glow which came from the Sacred Host.

At the altar, Caltro half-turned at the sudden commotion behind him. The hand holding the knife seemed to have stayed in its downward sweep. A sudden screech of fiendish rage rang through the room. The thing above the altar glared balefully down at him.

A malefic darkness seemed to spread from it, striking down against the Sacred

Host. Nayland felt as if an intolerable weight had been placed upon his arm. His muscles ached and his fingers began to shake. Out of the corner of his eye, he was aware of Blake and the doctor cowering in the doorway, their faces taut and fixed, their eyes wide and staring.

Then, with a neigh of anger, the creature at the end of the room began to twist and writhe as the light played over it, beating back the darkness. The aura of evil began to lessen.

Nayland found that he could breathe more easily. The strength returned to his arm and he was able to stand upright, squaring his shoulders. A moment later, the thing had vanished, the green light had snapped out of existence and only the pale candlelight from the altar showed in the room.

There was no sign of the Goat, nor of Caltro. The man had vanished as though he had never been. On the altar, Simon Merrivale stirred and tried to sit up, putting his hands to his head.

There was a vacant expression on his face. The rest of the men and women cowered against the wall, looking about them with frightened eyes. Nayland guessed that they would have nothing to fear from them. The nightmare and the terror had been temporarily removed.

'What happened?' asked the doctor shakily.

'They're gone now,' Nayland said. 'Do you think you could take a look at Merrivale, doctor? You may be able to do more for him now than we can.'

Shuddering a little from his recent ordeal, the doctor pushed his way forward towards the black stone altar. With an effort, Simon had pushed himself up on to one elbow. He grinned weakly as he saw them.

'Stephen! And you too, Richard. God, I never thought I'd see either of you again.'

'Just lie still for a moment,' said the doctor quietly. He seemed to have regained a little of his composure, but there was still a faint film of perspiration on his face and his eyes held a queer look as though he could still not understand what he had just witnessed.

'What happened to Caltro, Stephen?'

Blake asked finally, looking about him. 'I didn't see him leave when that horrible creature vanished, but I guess he must have done. You don't think we destroyed him too, do you?'

'I hope so. I sincerely hope so. But frankly, I doubt it. I believe he's still alive, somewhere, and that he'll come back as soon as the time is right. He almost succeeded then. I don't think his Evil Master will have killed him for that mistake.'

Blake nodded and walked forward, to the end of the altar. He bent and picked something up, bringing it back into the light. The mask and headdress of Shabaka. Without a word, he handed them to Nayland.

'Not very nice looking things, are they?' muttered Stephen with a slight laugh. Now that it was all over, he could feel some of the old confidence beginning to come back.

'What do you intend to do with these people?' asked the doctor, glancing up and jerking his head in the direction of the score of so people standing in little nervous groups round the room.

Nayland shrugged. It was something he hadn't considered before. Finally, he said. 'I don't think there's anything we can do with them — or for them. They made their choice a long time ago. Perhaps now they've seen that evil can be destroyed, they may change their minds about a lot of things. We'll leave them to make their own way home. I doubt whether we have anything to fear from them. They're mostly ignorant people who've got into this horrible affair so deeply that they can't get out.'

'Maybe hospital treatment,' suggested the other.

Nayland shook his head. 'I don't think that will be of any help to them. This isn't something that you can treat with drugs or electric shocks. This is evil incarnate, not a disease in the strict sense of the word. They don't believe that they're doing wrong. To them, it seems the most natural thing to do.'

'Nevertheless, it seems a terrible thing to do. To leave them with all — this.'

'They got themselves into this mess of

their own free will, doctor,' snapped Blake harshly. 'What about Simon?'

Reeves looked up from his examination. 'He'll be all right in the morning after a good night's sleep,' he said, stiffly. He shivered. 'Let's get out of this place,' he murmured. 'It gives me the creeps even though I know that the affair is finished.'

They walked out into the cold moonlight. The sky was clear overhead and there were a few stars just visible. The tall poplars bent and swayed in the wind. Behind them, the house lay silent with only a single flickering light in the window of one of the rooms.

In his right hand, Nayland carried the mask and feathered headdress, feeling a little quiver of revulsion at the touch of the cold skin against his fingers.

All that remained now, he thought, was to return these to their rightful place. He made up his mind to do that as soon as possible.

12

Lycanthrope!

The boat sailed on the evening tide, moving away from the land with a slow, steady motion that made it seem as though it was standing still and it was the land that moved away from them. Standing on the deck, leaning over the rail, Nayland glanced round at Blake and gave a grin.

'Now that we're on the last lap of the trip, I feel a little easier in my mind,' he said.

'If your guesses are anywhere near the truth, we ought to break the spell on this mask and headdress once it is handed back to Chalka's people.'

'That's right. But I've an idea that Caltro will try to lay his hands on them before that.'

'Caltro! But we saw him destroyed at that place outside Rodminster.'

'No, we only saw him vanish. I believe he left that place by some secret route he alone knew. The place must have been riddled with passages and it's more than likely that he escaped along one of them. Besides, I happen to know that he's still very much alive as are some of his closest followers.'

'How can you possibly know that?'

Nayland looked out at the sea for a long moment, before speaking. 'Tell me, Richard, did you have any impression that you were being followed just before we boarded the boat?'

Blake shook his head wonderingly.

'And what about you, Simon?'

Merrivale turned away from his contemplation of the land that now stood on the very rim of the horizon. 'I can't say I noticed anything like that, either,' he said.

'But who were they?' asked Blake.

'Some of Caltro's minions. I saw him once or twice and I've a suspicion that he's on board this ship, although I haven't seen him since we sailed.'

'You think he realises the power of these things we've got?'

Nayland nodded. 'I'm quite certain of it. You saw what happened when that woman touched the mask at the height of the ceremony. I doubt whether Caltro would have given them to her if he hadn't known of the voodoo associated with them.'

★   ★   ★

Nayland had remained up on deck after the others had gone down to their cabins. All around him in the darkness, the quietness stretched away to the far horizons.

For a long moment, he stood there, leaning over the rail, watching the water bubbling past, flashing in the moonlight. He had the weirdest idea that there were drums beating incessantly somewhere in the distance and presently he grew aware that this was nothing more than the thumping of his own pulse in his veins.

The next instant, he turned his head slightly, feeling eyes on him, and saw the dark figure standing in the shadows a little distance away. His first thought was that it was either one of the other passengers, or one of the crew on duty.

Then he saw the huge, balding head, gleaming whitely in the pale moonlight and he knew who it was.

'Caltro!' He half-whispered the name. The moon vanished into the cloud and for an instant he lost sight of the other.

Then it came out again and he saw that Caltro was less than three feet away, coming closer. He almost seemed to be gliding over the deck.

'Good evening, Mr. Nayland.'

'Mr. Caltro,' he said throatily. He felt afraid, but wasn't going to admit it in front of the other.

'I swore that night that we would meet again,' Caltro said, maliciously.

'I can't say that the feeling was mutual,' muttered Nayland. He leaned back against the rail. There was the faint booming of the water in his ears and in front of him — the leering face of Ernest Caltro, watching him closely, playing with him like a cat with a mouse. The other's close-set eyes flared briefly in his head like polished gems, matching the glitter of the moonlight on the sea.

Nayland felt a tiny shiver race along his spine. This man could almost pass as the Devil.

A sudden intuition warned him that this man was far more dangerous now than he had ever been before. The deep-set eyes bored into him, seeming to look right down into his very soul. They were twin red pools that held a peculiar flickering of malignant fire in their hellish depths.

'You have something I want, Nayland. I think you know what it is?'

'Simon Merrivale?'

'Bah! He is of no more use to me. Even his life would not appease the Great Master now. But with that mask which you have in your possession, I could have an unlimited power. Allied to the other forces I can control, there would be nothing to stand against me.'

'And you think I'll give it up to you as easily as that, even if I had it here?'

'You have it,' Caltro said. He laughed harshly. 'You have good cause to be afraid. Here, you are unprotected by those weapons you possessed that night. This time it shall not happen again. Either you give me the mask, or I drive you insane. Perhaps, I shall even destroy you.'

'The mask is back in England,' said Nayland feebly.

'Fool! I know why you are here. To take the relics back to Africa. With them in my possession, I can have all the power I need.'

'You'll never get them.'

'No?'

The other's features rippled in the moonlight, flowing like wax. Hell flared out of the slitted eyes. A shadow was beginning to move over Caltro's flabby features. He began to shrink a little, to shrivel up as he stood there.

Nayland recoiled with a sudden scream of horror. He knew now why Caltro was so sure he would get whatever he wanted.

Lycanthrope! So that was one of the powers possessed by this High Priest of Satan!

'No!' he screamed. 'Keep away from me.' He tried vainly to turn and run, but slipped on the smooth deck. The next instant, the thing that had been Ernest Caltro was upon him. Fangs clashed against his face. Claws caught him by the arms, sending thrills of pain surging madly along his limbs.

His mind was racing madly. Werewolves couldn't be killed. A bullet was no use against them. Only silver. The creature's weight pinned his arms effectively to his sides. Sharply pointed teeth gleamed above his throat, slavering a thin mist of hate.

Wildly, he struggled to get to his feet but one huge paw rested on his chest, crushing into his ribs. He felt as if his bones were about to snap and the air rushed out of his bursting lungs. Everything seemed to dissolve into a swarming blackness.

Feebly, desperately, he tried to pray, but the words were all confused, jumbled up so that they only made a hideous kind of sense. Dimly, above the roaring in his ears, he heard the tearing of cloth as the creature ripped the shirt away from his throat.

Then, almost before he was aware of it, the smashing pressure on his body eased. The pain in his chest lifted a little. Sobbing air into his aching lungs, he opened his eyes. He caught a vague glimpse of the werewolf dissolving into smoke, into thin air.

Caltro stood against the rail looking down at him with an expression of thwarted anger on his broad features. His lips were twisted into a snarl of bestial hatred. Then almost as swiftly as he had appeared, he vanished into the shadows along the deck.

Dazed, Nayland staggered to his feet and stood swaying for a moment clutching at the rail for support. He stared down at his body at the ragged tear in his shirt and saw the tiny, golden crucifix hanging on the end of its slender chain, glowing with a strangely icy fire in the moonlight.

Reaching his own room, he locked the door carefully behind him, went over to the mirror above the washbasin and stared into it at his reflection. There was a slight scratch on one cheek, but it hadn't bled very much, and another across his chest.

Taking off his jacket, he lay down on the bunk and closed his eyes. It was almost eleven o'clock and he was asleep almost before his head touched the pillow. His fatigue and the dull, almost hypnotic pounding of the waves beyond the porthole took precedence over everything else. He knew that he should have warned Simon and Blake, but he would do that first thing tomorrow. The horror that he had experienced on the deck had drained his energy.

That night, he had the first of the curiously haunting and disturbing dreams which were to be a regular occurrence for him during the voyage. Though he was to sleep soundly enough, he was never to be free of the dreams.

He dreamed that he was in a vast, dark place standing in the centre of a large clearing. Overhead there were the stars and a thin crescent moon. All around him were the trees of a jungle.

There was a fire in the middle of the clearing some distance away and figures crowded around it, prancing figures, carrying spears that shone in the firelight. As he listened in his dream, he could hear the weird, undulating chant rising from among them, but he could distinguish no words, for the language was not one that he knew.

Yet he had the feeling that he should know it and at times one or more of the natives would turn and stare at him almost accusingly as though he had been guilty of some breach of conduct. Then, leaping into the centre of the ring of light thrown by the fire, there came a strange, hideous creature, tall and grotesque, that shrieked and uttered strange cries.

Several seconds fled before he recognised the mask and headdress worn by the native. They were those he had in his possession. The dance continued, the natives whirling round and round the fire, stamping their feet in unison, waving their spears until there seemed to be a million flashes of light in the dark air above the fire.

Then, moving forward out of the shadows that ringed the others around, he saw the tall figure that darted forward, spear raised aloft.

The huge figure of the witchdoctor, as if forewarned, turned, but not quickly enough. The spear plunged downwards, the point driven deep into the other's flesh.

Nayland caught a glimpse of the contorted features of the slain man and heard the shrill scream of rage and agony; then he too screamed and woke.

He lay for some time trying to ascertain the reason for the dream. That it stemmed from his knowledge of these dark things, he knew and could not doubt; but how could he account for being a spectator at this scene? He hadn't played the part of an interloper, that much was certain.

Moreover, he had witnessed something that could only have been in his mind from what Chalka, the native had told him concerning the death of the witch-doctor Shabaka.

He lay for a long while, puzzling in vain over the problem. He had the idea that it was important but the only explanation he could credit at that moment lay in the work of a feverish and overworked imagination.

Lulled by the smooth movement of the ship, he drifted off into sleep once more and this time, his dream was sheer unadulterated nightmare, in which terrible things of blackness were pursuing him along empty streets and down narrow lanes towards an empty house that stood high upon the side of a hill with a single light showing in one of the windows.

There seemed to be lead weight attached to his feet so that he was unable to run and the creatures behind him padding forward on noiseless feet, came ever nearer until he could feel their hot breath on the back of his neck.

He threw a terrified glance over his shoulder as he ran and a cry burst from his lips as he saw the thing that was undeniably gaining on him with every minute.

A huge shape reared above his head and glared down at him with a malevolent hatred. A snake thing that had the face of a man and the features were terribly familiar. Ernest Caltro! He recognised the bloated face almost instantly. And then he saw the horns that protruded from the smooth forehead and the sharply pointed fangs that hung down from the corners of the mouth and he knew that it wasn't a man.

Madly, he hauled himself to his feet and floundered on through the clinging slime that stuck to his shoes. Chill water splashed against his legs, impeding him and the sound of the devil sliding after him sent a shiver of animal fear coursing through his body.

'Come back here, Stephen Nayland,' called the sexless, flat voice in his dream. 'You can't escape me now. No one escapes from the Evil Ones. Come back. It's useless to try to run away.'

The great, bloated head swooped down on the end of the long, glistening body, arching high in the air above him. Then it seemed to flash downwards like a striking snake, with an ugly vicious smile on the devilish features.

With a sudden convulsive effort, he

thrust himself forward into the mud, forcing his flagging muscles into terrified life. The flicking head missed his body by inches as he stumbled forward.

A splash of mud and ooze jetted into the air, then splashed down again all around him. There was a sharp, stabbing pain in his lungs and he found that it was becoming difficult to breathe properly. A red haze seemed to dance and sway in front of his eyes. An instant later, there was the sound of the monster gathering itself for another leap.

He stumbled forward for another few floundering steps. Then, without any warning, the ground suddenly fell away beneath him. His legs began to sink deeper into the ooze. Within seconds, it was up around his legs, climbing higher until it reached his waist. He could move no further, the mud holding him down as efficiently as the steel jaws of an animal trap.

He heard himself scream as he twisted his neck muscles and tried to look round at the thing behind him. It was virtually on top of him, sliding closer, moving with a tortuous motion as though striving to pull itself forward faster than nature had intended it to move.

The fanged mouth opened hungrily. Hell glared at him out of the slitted eyes that were so like those of Ernest Caltro. Inexorably, the mud began to climb up his body, dragging him down, holding him rigid, unable to move.

As it reached down to touch him, he had a last fading glimpse of it before he woke up, trembling, the sweat boiling out of his body.

13

Death in the Jungle

When the dawn came, brightening the eastern horizon, the fire in the middle of the small clearing, was little more than a heap of glowing embers. The jungle lay all around them, capricious and deadly, a menacing thing, full of vague twitterings and the crashing of nocturnal beasts fleeing from the oncoming daylight.

Stephen Nayland rolled over in his blankets, then sat up. He leaned across and woke Blake. With a swift, instinctive motion the other sat up, instantly awake.

'It's nearly dawn,' said Nayland unnecessarily. 'We'll start out again in an hour or so before the heat sets in. We ought to reach this village that Chalka spoke of by nightfall with a bit of luck.'

Blake nodded. He scrambled to his feet and stood looking about him. Then he kicked the fire into life and threw a handful of wood on to it until it had blazed up again. Less than ten feet away, Merrivale still lay in his blanket, his eyes closed. He was breathing quietly. Their guides were already awake, moving around in the brush.

Nayland shuddered at the memory of the nightmare journey to Africa. The trip on the boat had seemed never-ending. Day after day, he had expected Caltro to come back, to try to take the mask and headdress by force, but he hadn't put in any further appearances since that night on the boat deck.

One of the men came up to him, a troubled look on his face.

'There are men following us, bwana,' he said quietly. 'We see them before the sun rises. They're to the east, still in the jungle.'

'And they're coming this way?'

The guide nodded. 'They head for the village as we do,' he said sombrely.

'We'll break camp in twenty minutes,' Nayland called to the others. 'It looks as though we've got company whether we like it or not.'

'Caltro?' asked Blake.

'I think so. We'll have to go on the assumption that it is. There's no doubt why he's following us.'

★   ★   ★

They moved slowly forward down into the rocky valley, skirting the upthrusting thorn bushes and the last of the jungle trees. In a way, Nayland was sorry to be leaving the jungle behind. It meant coming out into the open where Caltro could see them, although they couldn't see him.

The guides went first, breaking the trail with Nayland following immediately behind, nursing his rifle in the crook of his arm. He kept one wary eye on the jungle behind them, although common sense told him that it would be impossible for him to pick out the other party if they kept well inside the fringe of trees.

The ground was uneven, dry and hard beneath their feet and they sank into the dust at every step. Through blurry lids, he saw Blake coming up along the column, his eyes red, but alert.

'We've just spotted the others coming out of the jungle,' he said tersely. 'They're gaining on us.'

Nayland stared into the haze behind him. Gradually, he was able to make out the details. There was a faint, half-seen movement on the edge of the jungle a couple of miles away and a moment later, he could just make out the small column of men winding out of the trees like a trail of ants.

'Get these porters moving,' he said half-angrily. There was the tension of fear in his voice. 'We've got to get to that village before Caltro overtakes us.'

Merrivale kept up a string of bitter comment as they pushed on as fast as possible, mostly it was barbed with resentment against the intolerable heat and the lazy natives. Nayland thrust his way forward with a strange, unflagging energy, maintaining an uneasy silence, too engrossed in his own thoughts for conversation.

They reached the lowermost foothills of the range with barely an hour of daylight left. Scrambling, sweating, slipping, they made their way into the jungle again, towards the native village. Here, it was a little easier to move. The trail was wider and most of the heat of the day had gone although some of it seemed to have been trapped by the trees and the canopy of leaves that closed in over their heads.

Somewhere behind them, probably only a quarter of a mile away, Nayland knew that Caltro was moving towards them, ready with some plan of his own to regain possession of the mask. If only he knew what the other intended to do.

Twenty minutes later, they entered the native village and stood in a little group while one of their guides explained their presence there.

'Can you understand what he's saying?' asked Blake.

Nayland nodded. 'He's telling the Chief that we've brought back the mask and headdress of Shabaka but that there are some men behind us who seek to take it away again.'

'That ought to stop Caltro, if anything can,' muttered Merrivale.

The talks between the guide and the native chief went on for the best part of fifteen minutes. When they were finished, the guide came back.

'The Chief says that you are all welcome to stay here in his village until you wish to return. He asks that you give the sacred relics back to him now.'

'Very well.' Nayland climbed to his feet and opened one of the packs. Taking out the mask and headdress, he handed them to the Chief.

'There will be much dancing and feasting in the village tonight,' said the guide. 'They are celebrating the return of — '

He broke off, his gaze fixed on something at the far end of the clearing. Nayland turned his head, guessing what he would see before he actually did so.

A small group of natives stepped into the clearing and behind them, grossly fat, came Caltro.

He walked forward confidently, supremely sure of himself. Nayland watched him curiously. There was a strange look on the other's face as he approached the Chief and said something to him, speaking rapidly in his own tongue.

'What's he saying?' asked Merrivale softly.

Nayland licked his lips. 'He's telling him that he's a powerful witchdoctor. That his spells are greater than any of those in the tribe, greater than Shabaka's and that unless the mask and headdress are given to him, he will curse everyone in the village. There will be no rain for the crops and a plague of locusts will destroy everything they now have.'

'He's bluffing,' muttered Merrivale.

Nayland shook his head. 'He isn't bluffing,' he said harshly. 'He can do everything he claims. I think the old Chief isn't so sure either. He looks undecided.'

'If he believes Caltro and gives him that mask, we're finished,' muttered Blake. He leapt forward, caught the guide by the arm and dragged him forward.

The Chief looked round in surprise as he saw them.

'Tell him that this man is a fake,' muttered Blake. 'That he can't do any of these things he claims.'

The guide muttered something harshly

to the Chief, who immediately turned on Caltro.

'He's telling him to prove his words,' said Nayland quietly, translating. 'This is what I've been afraid of all the time.'

In the centre of the clearing. Caltro drew a wide circle with a stick, tracing out the intricate pentagrams and heptagrams. Then he stood in the middle of them, holding his arms upraised, his face lifted towards the sky.

His lips were moving, uttering a string of gibberish that even Nayland couldn't understand. For a long moment, Caltro stood there as the darkness began to creep swiftly over the jungle. He snapped his fingers sharply several times.

The fire in the middle of the clearing, between the thatched huts suddenly sprang into life, the flames licking up into the heavens. There was a mutter from the natives. Overhead, the clouds were gathering swiftly, building up into a mass of darkness that blotted out the last rays of the setting sun.

Seconds later, there came a distant rumble of thunder, followed by another, louder and nearer. Lightning split the dark heavens, flashing high against the sky. There came another mutter from the gathering of superstitious natives.

Nayland could see that the old Chief was almost convinced. This was something he had never come up against before. Here was black magic such as he had never dreamed of.

So everything was lost, just when it seemed that they had defeated him, utterly and completely. So this was why Caltro hadn't bothered to make his move on the boat. He preferred to prove his power was far greater than theirs.

For a long minute there was silence in the clearing, a clinging silence such as Nayland had never known before. Deep inside, he had the impression that something was going to happen, something unforeseen.

Then, almost before he was aware of it, he saw the dark shadow materialise in the shelter of one of the huts. The face, as the native came out into the open, was covered with paint and for a moment Nayland thought it was Shabaka standing there, staring at them across the clearing, his right arm raised, the firelight shining redly on the tip of the upraised spear.

Nayland felt the muscles of his throat constrict. It was as if he had seen all of this enacted somewhere before, but he couldn't remember where. Then the memory came flooding back to him as he stood, rooted to the spot, unable to move.

That nightmarish dream he had had on board ship. Every detail here was almost the same as he had dreamed it that night. The fire blazing fiercely in the middle of the clearing. The natives huddled around it and the tall, grossly fat figure of Caltro standing in the middle of them all, picking up the mask and the headdress, holding them high above his head in an attitude of triumph.

But it was a triumph that was short-lived. The dark figure leapt into the clearing, face contorted. Caltro turned, seemed to catch a brief glimpse of the hate-distorted face that towered above his. Then the spear struck, knocking him to the ground.

The silence was shattered by a scream

that shrilled up and down a raw-edged scale, shrieking at their ears. A tremor ran along Nayland's limbs. Gradually, the shrieking sound died away into a gurgling that was even more horrible to hear.

When they went forward, there was only the crumpled figure of Caltro lying in the middle of the circle, his face upturned towards the sky so that the red glow from the fire fell full on it.

'God, what an expression,' muttered Merrivale. He turned away.

Caltro's eyes, wide and distended, looked as though they had seen something not fit for human eyes to witness.

The witchdoctor lowered his spear and, without a word, took the mask and headdress from the chief. Approaching the altar, he placed the relics carefully on the smooth stone and stepped back.

Raising his arms, he muttered something that Nayland couldn't understand. The next second there came a brilliant flash like a bolt of lightning from the heavens. When they could see clearly again the relics were gone — the shrine was empty!

'It's finished,' Nayland said in a low voice.

'But Caltro?' Merrivale put in. 'If it hadn't been for that spear in his chest, I'd swear he died of fright.'

Nayland nodded. 'My guess is that he did. When he saw the witchdoctor he was convinced it was Shabaka come to avenge himself on any who sought to defile his mask.'

THE END

We do hope that you have enjoyed reading this large print book.

Did you know that all of our titles are available for purchase?

We publish a wide range of high quality large print books including:
Romances, Mysteries, Classics
General Fiction
Non Fiction and Westerns

Special interest titles available in large print are:
The Little Oxford Dictionary
Music Book, Song Book
Hymn Book, Service Book

Also available from us courtesy of Oxford University Press:
Young Readers' Dictionary
(large print edition)
Young Readers' Thesaurus
(large print edition)

For further information or a free brochure, please contact us at:
Ulverscroft Large Print Books Ltd.,
The Green, Bradgate Road, Anstey,
Leicester, LE7 7FU, England.
Tel: (00 44) **0116 236 4325**
Fax: (00 44) **0116 234 0205**

SHERLOCK HOLMES AND THE GIANT'S HAND

Matthew Book

Three of the great detective's most singular cases, mentioned tantalisingly briefly in the original narratives, are now presented here in full. The curious disappearance of Mr Stanislaus Addleton leads Holmes and Watson ultimately to the mysterious 'Giant's Hand'. What peculiar brand of madness drives Colonel Warburton to repeatedly attack an amiable village vicar? Then there is the murderous tragedy of the Abernetty family, the solving of which hinges on the depth to which the parsley had sunk into the butter on a hot day . . .

EXCEPT FOR ONE THING

John Russell Fearn

Many criminals have often believed that they'd committed the 'Perfect Crime', and blundered. Chief Inspector Garth of Scotland Yard is convinced that modern science gives the perfect crime even less chance of success. However, Garth's friend, scientist Richard Harvey, believes he can rid himself of an unwanted fiancée without anyone discovering what became of the corpse. Yet though he lays a master-plan and uses modern scientific methods to bring it to fruition, he makes not one but several mistakes . . .